Believer on Tour

Taz

Stephen Arterburn
with Angela Hunt

Tyndale House Publishers, Inc.
Wheaton, Illinois

Visit Tyndale's exciting Web site at www.tyndale.com

Visit the Young Believer Web site at www.youngbeliever.com

The song "Rock" on page 145 is copyright © 2003 by Word Music, Inc. (ASCAP), Silerland Music (ASCAP), and Dayspring Music, Inc. (BMI). All rights on behalf of itself and Silerland Music administered by Word Music, Inc. Used with permission.

The song "Go Vertical" on page 153 is copyright © 2003 by Word Music, Inc. (ASCAP) and Silerland Music (ASCAP). All rights on behalf of itself and Silerland Music administered by Word Music, Inc. Used with permission.

The song "Your Word" on page 155 is copyright © 2003 by Word Music, Inc. (ASCAP), Silerland Music (ASCAP), and Nick Trevisick Songs (ASCAP). All rights administered by Word Music, Inc. Used with permission.

Scripture quotations are taken from the *Holy Bible*, New Living Translation, copyright © 1996. Used by permission of Tyndale House Publishers, Inc., Wheaton, Illinois 60189. All rights reserved.

Library of Congress Cataloging-in-Publication Data

Arterburn, Stephen, date.
    Taz / Stephen Arterburn and Angela Elwell Hunt.
      p. cm. — (Young believer on tour ; 6)
    Summary: Twenty-year-old Taz, African American sound engineer for the all-white-teenaged YB2, questions his sense of belonging.
    ISBN 0-8423-8340-9 (sc)
    [1. Musical groups—Fiction. 2. Bands (Music)—Fiction. 3. African Americans—Fiction. 4. Traffic accidents—Fiction. 5. Christian life—Fiction] I. Hunt, Angela Elwell, date. II. Title.
    PZ7.A74357Taz 2004
    [Fic]—dc22   2004000007

Printed in the United States of America

10 09 08 07 06 05 04
7   6   5   4   3   2   1

I'm living in a world gone crazy,

What once was black is blue,

The future sure looks hazy,

What am I supposed to do?

White is black and black is blue

And blue is always something new—

Colors of a world gone mad.

Colors of a world gone sad.

—Paige Clawson and Shane Clawson

FROM "COLORS"
YB2 MUSIC, INC.

January 1

YB2 TO PERFORM AT ROSE BOWL HALFTIME SHOW

By Stella Cox, Los Angeles Register

On this New Year's Day in Pasadena, California, sports fans cling to their tickets while alumni of Ohio State and the University of Oklahoma hold tight to their hotel reservations throughout the Los Angeles area. But another event on the program is responsible for a last-minute surge in ticket scalping, and the people desperately seeking tickets aren't sports fanatics or faithful alumni. They are teens and preteens, and their fascination with the Rose Bowl springs from the scheduled appearance of YB2, pop's latest and most successful band.

YB2 was originally scheduled to appear in the Rose Bowl parade, but last month security chiefs nixed that appearance. In November, Paige Clawson, the group's pianist and daughter to group director Ron Clawson, was abducted at the Macy's Thanksgiving Day parade. Understandably reluctant to invite even more stringent security measures, Rose Bowl officials cancelled the singers' parade appearance and gave them the coveted halftime show slot instead.

Along with the Ohio State University marching band and the famed "Pride of Oklahoma" band, YB2 will perform a medley of contemporary hits, including "Never Stop Believin'" and "Y B Alone?" Publicist Rhonda Clawson says that the show will be "fresh and original, with something to please everyone. Our team has been working hard on the new arrangements, and they can't wait to perform with two wonderful college bands."

YB2 leapt from obscurity to the top of the charts two years ago when Ron Clawson introduced his children, Shane and Paige, to the music industry along with singers Noah Dudash, a native Californian, Liane Nelson, and newcomer Josiah Johnson. Since the debut of their first album, the teens from YB2 have sung and danced their way into American pop culture.

When asked if he favored the Ohio State Buckeyes or the Oklahoma Sooners, band member

Noah Dudash replied, "Both are great teams from great schools. We're just happy to be in the middle of all the excitement, dude."

Spoken like a true Californian.

Saturday, January 1

Josiah Johnson clenched his hands as he stood onstage before the roaring crowd and hoped no one would notice that his kneecaps were wobbling beneath his jeans. Surely no one could tell, especially from the distance of the stands, but some of the photographers had lenses that looked about three feet long.

He always got hoppy-knees when he was nervous. Liane said her heart thumped so hard it jiggled the cross necklace she wore in performances, and Shane said a bad case of nerves always made his hands sweat. Josiah didn't know if any of the others suffered from jumpy kneecaps, and so far he'd been too embarrassed to ask.

He bent his knees slightly to relax his legs as the marching bands' bass drums pounded. The members of YB2 had spent the last two days rehearsing this number with a tape, and the drums hadn't sounded this powerful on the recording. The pounding pulse was enough to make his knees start dancing again—

But here came his cue and he had to move.

He pivoted in the choreographed step, turning sideways, then lifted his head and raised his arm toward the crowd as Shane stepped out from the back line and began to rap "Come On." And though the microphones they wore were powerful, the roar from the crowd nearly swallowed up Shane's words:

"Some people ask us why we spend our time,
Singing songs with occas'nal retro themes,
They can't seem to feel the rhythm and rhyme,
There's an ancient pulse behind everything,
Life's greatest gifts are as old as the sky,
Love and laughter come to us from above,
Every good and great thing that meets the eye,
Spills from the bounty of the Father's love."

Josiah felt his knees relax as he moved with the others and sang the chorus:

"We (we) want to reach back into the past,
Grab what is good and celebrate life,
We (we) want to make the good things last,
Use them to reflect the True Light.
So come on and take me by the hand,
Come on, it's time to take your stand,
Come on, I'll lead you into the land
Where dreams become reality . . ."

In a specially choreographed move during the instrumental break, Josiah and the others swung their arms out in a wide half circle. He and Noah pointed to the Ohio State band dressed in scarlet and gray; Liane and Shane pointed to the band from the University of Oklahoma in crimson and cream. The college musicians took the lead and played the melody, trumpets screeching, tubas bellowing, and flutes singing as the fans roared. Josiah never knew college bands could generate as much excitement as football teams, but the fans in the stands went wild as the musicians dueled it out, one band playing one phrase, then the other answering.

Josiah wished he could stand still and watch the action, but he and the others had moves of their own to perform. He began the quick side step, moving in perfect position along with Liane and Shane and Noah, then turned with an arm spin—

Brother. The button on his sleeve caught the stage microphone hanging from his ear, dragging it from its place. Josiah could feel the pressure of the thin wire on the back of his neck, which meant the mouthpiece was probably dangling somewhere on his chest. The heavy battery pack was still clipped to the waistband of his jeans, but the part that mattered was far away from his mouth . . . and he had to sing a solo in about thirty seconds.

What could he do?

He glanced toward Noah, hoping to catch his eye, but Noah was grinning at the crowd and totally into the performance. Liane was moving just past Noah, but there was no way Josiah could get her attention without breaking formation and totally ruining the choreography. If he did that, a half dozen television cameras would record his mistake, and thousands of people watching at home would think YB2's newest member was nothing but a klutz.

Whatever happens, keep going as if nothing's wrong. The cardinal rule of show business had been drummed into his head ever since he'd joined YB2. If the power goes off, if you get a lump in your throat, if you forget the words, just keep going. Don't stop. Don't make a face. Don't ruin it for the others by calling attention to yourself.

But what was he supposed to do? He had no mike, and in a minute he'd have to open his mouth and the entire world would know something terrible had happened.

He glanced up, automatically searching the crowd for Taz's familiar face at the soundboard, but there *was* no soundboard at the Rose Bowl. The audio people were sitting up in a glass-walled booth along with the TV people, and Taz wasn't even working this gig. The responsibility for this show lay in the hands of a television crew, and most of them were too busy watching the cheerleaders to even notice that Josiah had lost his microphone.

He turned again, keeping up with the choreography, then felt his kneecap shudder when an unexpected sound caught his ear: *pssst!* He looked toward the edge of the platform and saw Taz standing there, a grin on his face and a handheld cordless microphone in his grip.

Josiah nearly melted in relief. Nodding ever so slightly to show that he understood, he finished the set of moves, then broke out of line just long enough to take two giant steps and reach Taz.

"City street newsboy yells out the bad news," he rapped, the new microphone secure in his hand,
"CNN broadcasts grief, gloom, and despair,
People hunker down behind their closed doors,
Been so long since they have lifted a prayer,
God's still great and he is still on his throne,
Evil can never gain the upper hand,
If we call out we'll get a clear dial tone,
God's line is faster than the hottest broadband . . ."

Still clinging to the mike, he stepped back into line with the others, then took a second to glance toward the side of the platform. Taz still stood there, arms crossed, his smile gleaming in the bright lights.

Thank goodness for a soundman who paid attention.

Josiah sang on.

2

"Man, I can't thank you enough," Josiah said, falling into step beside Taz as they hurried through a tunnel leading out of the stadium.

Taz grinned. "It was nothing, Joe. I saw your mike fly off and I knew you had that solo coming up. If I hadn't been there, I figure you just would have picked up your mike and adjusted it. No biggie."

"It *was* a biggie—I never can get those little mikes to hang right, and I would've looked like a loser trying to put it back in place. You've got the gift, man."

Taz snorted as if Josiah had just told the biggest lie in the world, but Josiah knew it was the truth. Even if Taz had been feeling unnecessary among all the bigwig network guys who ran the audio for the Rose Bowl, his quick thinking sure saved YB2 and Josiah from a ton of embarrassment.

Shane, who walked in front of Josiah, turned to look over his shoulder. "Man, I wish we could stay and see the rest of the game."

"You just want to watch the cheerleaders," Liane answered, elbowing him. "Come on, RC's waiting."

They found RC and Aunt Rhonda in the YB2 dressing room, and both adults wore huge smiles as the singers entered. "You all did great." RC threw an arm around Paige as she entered. "Absolutely super!"

"It was cool," Noah said, enduring an embrace from Aunt Rhonda. "We should do football games more often."

RC shook his head. "I'm glad we don't. Too complicated since each game is different. If we had to learn special arrangements for every halftime show, we'd never get a production on the road."

Aunt Rhonda glanced at her watch, then clapped her hands together. "Speaking of the road, guys, we have to hit it. If we don't leave in the next twenty minutes, we're going to be stuck in traffic like you've never seen. So go get out of those performance clothes and get this stuff packed up. We've got a plane waiting."

Josiah followed Shane and Noah into the curtained cubicle where their street clothes lay scattered around a pair of benches, then he unbuttoned his shirt. A grin crept over his face as he thought about the ride home. The best perk of this gig was the chartered jet. The sleek white plane had picked them up in Orlando, the group's home base, and flown them nonstop to an airport in Los

Angeles. The pilot was waiting now to take them back to Orlando.

Josiah slipped out of his shirt and thought about where he'd be if he hadn't signed on with YB2 six months before—he'd probably be home, bored and stretched out on the couch while his dad watched the Rose Bowl and his mother took down Christmas decorations.

Yessir, life with YB2 sure had its high points.

3

Taz tried to keep a smile off his face as RC praised him for his quick action during the halftime performance. "Taz was alert, which is what all of you should be at all times," RC said, moving down the aisle as he passed out sheets of paper on the jet. "Of course, it'd help a lot if we could have those microphones surgically implanted or something so they wouldn't come off."

"Sorry about that, RC." Josiah looked up, his eyes full of worry, but they cleared when RC shook his head with a smile.

"Don't worry about it, Joe. These things happen. And you were working with new choreography, so I imagine it couldn't be helped."

Taz scanned the sheet of paper Liane passed him, then realized he was holding a copy of the group's January

Taz

itinerary. They'd taken two weeks off at Christmas, returned to a hectic two days of rehearsal to prepare for the Rose Bowl, and tomorrow morning they would board the bus and take off for nine days of nonstop travel. Their first concert gig would be January 3 at the Mobile Convention Center in Mobile, Alabama.

He whistled softly as he looked at the schedule. What a way to start the year! A few of the gigs had been scheduled back-to-back, which meant they'd be sleeping on the bus a lot.

"As you can tell—" RC settled into one of the jet's backward facing seats—"it's going to be a busy month. But there are highlights—the Mobile concert is sold out because the promoter spent a fortune on advertising. The New Orleans and Dallas concerts should be sold out by the time we arrive."

"I see we're traveling mostly in the South." Liane lifted her chin. "Is that because of the weather?"

Aunt Rhonda nodded. "You bet. Larry's a great driver, but we don't want to take a chance on snow-covered interstates. We're going to try to stay in the South and Southwest for the next three months."

RC set his itinerary aside and folded his hands as he looked at the group members. "I'm kinda glad I have you all together like this," he said, grinning. "And since it's going to take us a few hours to get back to Florida, I thought this might be a good time to do a little personal sharing." He lifted a brow. "We've been so rushed since you all got back from Christmas break that we haven't had much time to talk as a team. So—anybody want to tell us how you spent your Christmas vacation?"

Taz looked around at the others. He knew how Shane had spent his vacation because he and Shane had experienced a crash course in basketball at the Clawson house. Aunt Rhonda had brought in a star college player named Inbae Kim to help Shane with a few basics, and Shane had worked with Inbae on his singing.

Josiah waved his hand. "I spent most of my time with my parents and my sisters. I thought I'd spend a lot of time with my best friend, Aaron, but things felt weird when I was home." He looked down at the floor and shrugged. "I wanted things to be normal, the way they were before, but all Aaron wanted to do was talk about all the places I've been and the famous people I've met. He still wanted to come over, but things felt . . . strange. It was like he was expecting me to be someone different, you know?"

Liane nodded. "I know what you mean. Every time I go home, I spend more and more time with my parents and less time with my friends. I don't want to avoid them, but it's like they're not comfortable around me anymore. I noticed it last Christmas and last summer, so this Christmas I kinda laid low and just sat around the house and watched movies. Oh—and I went shopping." Her eyes twinkled as she smiled. "Mom and I still like to shop."

"So I've noticed." Noah laughed. "I saw that you brought a new suitcase back with you."

Liane crossed her arms. "I had to. My old one was worn out."

"It was too small, you mean. You couldn't get all your stuff into it."

"Okay, okay." RC held up his hands before their good-natured ribbing could turn into a war of words. Taz said nothing but silently chewed his gum as he grinned at Noah and Liane. Noah was right about Liane's collection of "stuff," but Taz understood why she wanted to carry a lot with her. He liked stuff too, but he was into gadgets instead of clothes and makeup. Every time he read about a new electronic gizmo, he wanted to try it out. And if it turned out to be something he could use for the group, well, that was great. In the last six months he'd discovered new stage microphones that were practically invisible from the audience, and the guys were still raving about the Game Boy Advance SPs he'd found a couple of years ago. There were hotter game players on the market now, but the Game Boys were backwards compatible, allowing the guys to play practically any Game Boy game on the market. They also came in really cool colors.

"I didn't do much over Christmas," Shane said, joining the discussion. He grinned at Taz. "Taz and I just hung out with the number one college basketball player in the nation, who taught us a few tricks. That pretty much rocked."

Noah slipped lower in his seat and crossed his arms. "I'm so jealous, dude."

"It was cool having Inbae around," Paige added. "I didn't play ball, but I helped Aunt Rhonda design the gym. And my mom came in for a couple of days after Christmas. It was nice to see her."

An awkward silence followed this announcement, and Taz felt himself feeling sorry for Paige and Shane. Their mother had left the family soon after Paige was born. Nobody ever said so, but Taz thought maybe the woman couldn't cope with raising a blind girl. But blindness had never stopped Paige. And Shane and Paige had a great home with RC and his sister, Rhonda. Shane and Paige didn't see their mom much, but she did come to Orlando every now and then.

Taz lowered his eyes as he thought of his own parents. His mother had spent most of December in New York, where his grandmother had been ill—congestive heart failure, the doctors called it. When she died the day after Christmas, Taz flew up for the funeral and then flew with his mom back home to Orlando. His dad, a soldier stationed in Bosnia as part of a UN peacekeeping force, hadn't been able to come home at all for the holiday.

Taz tried to tell himself it didn't matter. After all, he wasn't a kid—he was twenty years old, a full-grown adult. He had a pretty big position as YB2's sound engineer, and he was making good money. In a few years he'd have enough experience to open his own recording studio, then he would settle down, maybe get married and raise a family . . . but right now he was having too much fun.

Noah leaned into the aisle and smiled at the other singers. "I went surfing nearly every day on my break."

Liane pretended to shiver. "Didn't you *freeze*?"

"Yeah, the water was cold, so I wore a wet suit. But when you're on the beach, man, you just gotta go for it."

RC looked around the group before his eyes met Taz's for a moment. "Anyone else want to share?"

Taz lowered his gaze, knowing RC wouldn't press if he didn't want to speak.

Sometimes he felt a little awkward with the group—he was part of them, no doubt about that, but he wasn't really one of them. He wasn't a singer, so he didn't perform onstage, he didn't have performance clothes, and he wasn't in any of the group posters or publicity shots. He was also black, while everyone else was white, yet nobody in the group made an issue of skin color.

Still, even though his job separated him from the others, he traveled everywhere with them, he was involved in all team meetings and decisions, and he made as much money as the singers. RC had never been cheap; he paid well, especially when the group's success skyrocketed.

"Okay, then." RC slapped his knees. "Let's enjoy the flight home and try to get some rest. We'll be leaving tomorrow afternoon at 2:00 sharp, so when we get back from church, make sure you pack for at least ten days out. This is going to be a busy tour, so we might as well settle in and prepare for it."

The meeting broke up in a noisy babble. Liane and

Shane stood and walked toward the back of the plane where a tiny fridge had been stocked with fruit juice and soft drinks. Across the aisle from Taz, Josiah pressed his forehead to the rectangular window. "Hey," he called, his voice ringing with excitement, "is that the Grand Canyon down there?"

Taz leaned toward his own window and looked down on a brown and orange and pink landscape unlike anything he'd ever seen in Florida.

How cool was that?

4

Sunday, January 2

Josiah was one of the first singers out of the van when they arrived back at the house from church. While the others headed toward the kitchen where Aunt Rhonda would soon spread a huge lunch, he hurried to the room he shared with Noah.

He'd begun to pack last night, but he wasn't quite finished. He still had to make sure he had enough under-wear to last ten days. Though he *could* do laundry on the road, the last time he'd tried, he'd turned all his socks and underwear pink. And he wanted to toss a notebook into his bag in case he wanted to write a letter home.

His suitcase lay open on the bed; his mostly empty backpack lay next to it. He pulled his laptop from the desk, then closed the lid and slid it into the bag along with the plug and an extra battery. He tossed in his Game Boy Advance SP and a pack of playing cards. Most of the

Taz

guys preferred playing their Game Boys, but sometimes the girls convinced them to play rummy or crazy eights. Josiah had to admit that playing cards with the girls was more fun than staring at a video screen alone.

He found a half-used spiral notebook in the desk drawer, then tossed it into the backpack, too. He and his parents sent e-mails every couple of days, but over the break his mom had hinted that she'd enjoy a snail-mail letter, too. "You can hang on to a paper letter," she'd said. "You can stick it in your purse and carry it with you. And when you send me that letter, Joey, you could enclose some pictures, too."

Josiah had tried to point out that she could always print out an e-mail and even a digital photograph, but his mother had grown up in a time when computers were huge beige boxes in laboratories, not little machines that cluttered desktops and kitchen counters.

So . . . maybe he would write her a letter or two. Sometimes you had to bend a little to please your parents.

He found his favorite gym shoes under the bed and tossed them into the suitcase, then zipped up the bag and took a last look around the room. The bed was still unmade, but this time Aunt Rhonda wouldn't care if they left their room a mess. She always had the housekeeper strip the sheets after they left on tour, so it would make no sense to make the bed now.

He paused before zipping up his book bag. The sight of his little silver Game Boy reminded him that Nintendo had just released a new WWF wrestling game. He'd seen a zillion commercials for the game over the break, and the graphics looked absolutely awesome. He'd give anything to be the first in the group to have it—it was sure to make the long hours on the bus fly by.

He glanced at the clock on the nightstand. One o'clock, so if he didn't eat lunch he'd still have time to get to the store. He had money, too, a handful of ten-dollar bills left over from his YB2 Christmas bonus. The only thing he needed was a ride to Target or Best Buy.

Shane was the only YB2 member old enough to drive, but he was still eating and there was no way he'd willingly miss a meal. RC wouldn't want to go to the store when he was trying to get the bus packed, and Aunt Rhonda would be too busy taking care of lunch and overseeing last-minute details before they pulled out.

Liane had no driver's license. Paige was blind.

Which left Taz as a possible driver. If he was packed, if he didn't mind getting up from lunch, and if he wouldn't mind taking a little side trip.

A lot of ifs. Still, it never hurt to ask.

Josiah stuffed his wallet into his pocket, then hurried down the hall. The kitchen buzzed with activity as the members of YB2 filled their plates with barbequed chicken, potato salad, coleslaw, and potato chips.

"Joe," Aunt Rhonda called, spotting him. "Get on in here. You'd better hurry or there won't be anything left."

"Actually," Josiah looked around, "I was hoping someone might want to make a quick run to the Target up the road. I want to pick something up before we leave."

The chatter around the table stopped for a moment, then Josiah looked at Taz. "Taz? You up for a trip?"

Taz turned to RC. "Um . . . am I?"

RC pursed his lips for a moment. "You're all packed, right?"

Taz nodded. "The equipment's all stacked in the garage. The minute Larry pulls in, it can go on the bus."

"Okay, then." RC pulled a set of keys from his pocket, then tossed them to Taz. "Take the Z4. And be careful."

Taz's grin widened. "You sure you want to trust me with this machine?"

RC nodded. "Yeah—I think the van's low on gas. But you guys be quick, okay? Larry will be here soon and we need to get loaded before two."

Josiah struggled to contain his excitement as he looked around the room. "Anybody else need anything from Target? I'll pick it up for you."

With her mouth full of food, Liane waved, holding Josiah's attention until she could swallow. "Yes," she finally said, "I need some lip gloss. Any brand, but red. And a true red, not an orange red."

Josiah looked at Taz. "You know the difference between true red and orange red?"

"I think so." Taz pocketed the keys. "Anybody else need anything?"

When no one else answered, Taz nodded. "Okay, then. See you guys in a few minutes."

5

Taz put the BMW Roadster in gear and grinned as the engine purred under the hood. "Man," he murmured, not caring whether Josiah heard or not, "this is one *fine* car!"

Still a little amazed that RC had trusted him with his favorite vehicle, Taz backed out of the garage and turned the two-seater toward the street. He'd been extra careful not to brush up against the car in the garage, and cautious even when he slipped the key into the ignition. RC didn't have many opportunities to drive this baby, and the vehicle was clean—absolutely spotless—without a scratch inside or out.

Taz heard the creak of the leather as he settled back in the seat. If he worked hard and saved his money, someday he might own a car like this.

Beside him, Josiah sat with one hand propped on the

door, the other on the back of Taz's seat. The warm
Florida sun spilled over them, sparkling the silver-gray
paint on the convertible's hood and warming the leather
trim on the steering wheel.

Taz shifted into drive, then eased down on the accel-
erator. The engine responded like a team of well-bred
horses.

"Wow." Josiah grinned. "I can't believe RC let you
take the Z!"

"Me neither." Taz pulled onto the residential street,
then drove toward the main entrance of the gated subdivision. "How cool is this?"

They had pulled on their favorite baseball caps and
sunglasses before leaving the house—a precaution all
members of YB2 had learned to take before going out in
public—but Taz knew he would have felt like someone
special in this car even if he'd never joined YB2. The car
drew stares from everyone they passed—other drivers
and pedestrians.

After leaving the subdivision, they pulled up to an
intersection with a six-lane highway and stopped. While
they waited for the light to change, Taz tugged on the
brim of his Tampa Bay Buccaneers cap, then turned on
the radio and pressed the presets, searching for a good
station.

He really didn't care what they listened to. Up
ahead, past the intersection, he could see the huge
circular logo of the Target store, so this ride would end
all too soon.

He glanced at Josiah. "What did you need to get at Target?"

"You mean . . . besides a true red lip gloss?"

"Yeah, besides that."

A guilty expression entered Josiah's eyes. "Um . . . I wanted to pick up a WWF game for the Game Boy Advance. I know that sounds selfish, but Shane will like it too. I figured we could all share it on the bus."

Taz rested his arm on the driver's door. "Hey, man, I don't care what you wanted to get. It's not like you're causing a problem or anything."

Josiah tilted his head, then smiled. "Yeah. It's no problem."

"And you're gonna let me play it, too, right?"

Josiah's smile broadened. "You bet."

"Then it's cool. If we don't get back in time to eat, I'll throw some food in a plastic bag and take it on the bus."

Taz nodded in time to a hip-hop beat that rumbled through the stereo speakers. Life was good. Here he was, riding in a sizzling hot car on a beautiful January day . . .

The light changed. Taz pressed on the gas, then put both hands on the wheel as the Z4 sprang forward. He grinned at Josiah, then glanced over his shoulder to prepare for a right turn into the Target parking lot.

His eyes swept the car; he saw the stopped traffic on the highway and nothing but empty asphalt behind him. But when his gaze passed back over Josiah's face, the kid's eyes had opened to the size of dinner plates and suddenly the car was moving *sideways*, not forward.

Deafening sounds filled his ears—a crunch and clatter and roar—and someone was screaming and then the world went dark and light and dark and light again as the car rolled and Taz's glasses flew from his nose. His head hit the gearshift, Josiah's elbow smacked his face, and then the world went dark, dark, and Taz felt himself falling into a black hole he had not seen approaching.

6

Liane had just taken the last Krispy Kreme from the box when the phone rang. Ignoring the ringing telephone, Aunt Rhonda lifted a brow in Liane's direction. "You know," she said evenly, "I'll give you ten dollars for that doughnut."

Liane laughed softly. Everyone knew about Aunt Rhonda's addiction to Krispy Kremes, and no one took her offers seriously. "Why, Aunt Rhonda," she answered, widening her eyes in a look of mock innocence, "you wouldn't send me away from the table without dessert, would you?"

Aunt Rhonda made a face, then leaned forward on the counter and propped her chin in her hand. "Actually, Lee, I was hoping you wouldn't eat that because—well, I think it's old. It's left over from breakfast, for heaven's sake. If

Taz

you'll just let me have it, I'll make sure Larry stops at a Krispy Kreme place after you guys head out."

"Nice try, Aunt Rhonda, but you're not getting my doughnut." To make her point, Liane lifted the pastry high, then took a huge bite out of the bottom of the sugared circle.

"I guess I'll just have to suffer, then." Sighing dramatically, Aunt Rhonda straightened and reached for the ringing telephone. "Hello?"

With her dessert in a firm grasp between sugary fingers, Liane propped her arms on the table and looked around the room. Larry Forsyth, the bus driver, had arrived and was enjoying a cup of coffee. RC was reading the Sunday paper while he finished a heaping plate of potato salad, and Noah had gone to his room to finish packing. Shane had left the kitchen too, probably to toss a few more clothes into his suitcase, but Paige lingered at the kitchen bar, sipping her Coke with an absent expression on her face.

Liane had come to know that look well. Paige had the crazy ability to block life's noise and commotion out of her mind, and she was probably composing a new song or dreaming about some sort of symphony.

Liane sometimes wished she could do the same thing. Taking another bite of the doughnut, she looked at Aunt Rhonda, who was now holding the phone to her ear with one hand while she covered her free ear with the other. A worry wrinkle had crept between the woman's brows, and the color had drained from her face.

Liane stopped chewing. This had to be bad news for somebody.

As tension radiated from Aunt Rhonda, silence spread through the room like a fog. RC looked up from his paper, Larry stopped slurping his coffee. Even Paige lifted her head and turned toward Aunt Rhonda with a questioning look on her face.

"Where?" Aunt Rhonda's voice came out hoarse, as if she had forced it through a tight throat. She lifted her gaze from the kitchen counter and looked straight at RC.

"Okay," she finally said, nodding as if the person on the phone could see her. "We're on our way."

She hung up, then pressed both hands to the countertop as if her knees had suddenly gone wobbly. "It's the boys." She looked from RC to Larry, the only other adult in the room. "Taz and Josiah. They were in an accident right outside the Target parking lot. A truck or something ran a red light and smacked right into them."

Liane looked to RC, whose throat moved in a sudden swallow. "Are they all right?"

"He—the policeman on the phone—didn't know. He said they were being airlifted to Orlando Regional Medical, to the trauma center. We need to go. They need someone to sign consent forms. And I have the medical consent forms for Josiah, so I'll need to take those down—"

"I'll go." RC stood, letting the newspaper slide to the floor as he hesitated, one hand going to his head. "I'll take the forms, but you need to stay here and call their parents, Ro." He looked at his sister, and for the first time ever Liane saw honest fear in the director's eyes. "Call them, give them the hospital's number. Taz's mother can come straight over, but Josiah's parents—"

"I'll call them." Aunt Rhonda turned slowly, as if she had suddenly aged thirty years. "And I'll go to the hospital as soon as I've finished. I'll have my cell phone if you need me."

Larry stood as RC moved toward the door. "You'd better let me drive, Ron."

RC nodded absently.

"Dad?" Paige turned toward him. "Can we come?"

RC hesitated only a moment. "Yeah. Come on—we'll take the van."

Without thinking, Liane slipped off her bar stool and hurried to the foyer. "Noah! Shane!" she yelled, grabbing her purse from where it waited with her luggage by the door. "Come out here *now*! We're going to the hospital!"

7

Noah leaned against the seat in the second row of
the van and studied RC's face. The man rode in the front
passenger seat, but his face had taken on an expression
Noah had never seen him wear. His eyes had gone narrow
and tense with worry and his mouth was set in a straight
line, though a quiver rippled through his jaw every couple
of minutes. Larry drove the van like he drove the bus—
with purpose and a look-out-here-we-come attitude that
made Noah double-check his seat belt.

Paige sat silently on the seat beside him, her face
smooth and still, like the news hadn't yet sunk in.
Liane sat next to Paige and stared out the front wind-
shield, wincing each time they changed lanes or passed
another car.

They had to drive by the intersection near Target as

they drove to the hospital, but Larry didn't linger at the light. He turned right onto the highway as soon as the traffic cop let him through, but the van was held up long enough for Noah to see RC's beloved sports car—or what was left of it—in the center of the median. Blue and red lights flashed from three police cruisers. One cop stood in the intersection and directed traffic, while another was helping a man hook the front end of a battered SUV to a tow truck.

Noah saw RC's eyes flicker toward the crumpled sports car, then he turned his head and pressed his hand over his mouth. Noah knew he wasn't upset about the car—RC had insurance, and even without it he could afford to buy another Z4. RC had to be thinking what Noah guessed they were all thinking—how could two guys survive an accident that left the car looking like a twisted soft drink can?

Noah heard a sob rip from Liane's throat as Larry turned the corner. "What?" he mouthed to her, careful not to break the silence.

Her lip quavered as her gaze met his. "His hat," she whispered. "I saw Taz's Buccaneers cap in the road."

Noah closed his eyes and looked away. For a moment he'd almost been able to believe that Josiah and Taz could have walked away from the mangled car in the median. He'd been hoping they'd get to the hospital to find that all their fear was for nothing, that through the miracle of seat belts and the BMW's rollover protection system, they hadn't been hurt at all.

But Taz would never, *ever* willingly leave his Buccaneers cap in the road.

They rode in silence for another fifteen minutes, then Larry turned the van into the hospital parking lot and pulled under a covered driveway. "You all can get out here," he said, turning in the seat. "I'll go find a place to park. You guys need to be inside."

After thanking him, RC climbed out of the front seat while the girls, Noah, and Shane followed. The singers walked without speaking as RC approached the glass doors to the emergency room. They halted when he turned at the last minute.

"I'm glad you are all here," he said, his face pale. "But I don't want you to see the guys until we know exactly what happened. I'd like you all to go to the waiting room and sit tight until we know something definite. I'll fill you in as soon as I know what's going on."

Noah stepped back as Shane nodded to his father. Without another word, RC opened the double doors, then hurried toward a reception desk while Shane led the others to an area filled with rows of plastic bucket chairs.

Noah sat down in a chair next to the wall while Liane slipped into the seat next to him. "I can't believe it," she whispered, tears slipping from her lashes. "This is so terrible."

"We don't know that it's terrible," Noah pointed out. "We don't know anything."

She exhaled sharply. "Noah, didn't you see that car?"

He had, but he didn't want to think about what would

have happened if he'd been sitting in that car when the SUV struck it. He couldn't even imagine what Taz and Josiah had gone through.

Shane guided Paige to one of the chairs across from Noah, then helped her sit down. He sat next to her, but he perched on the edge of his seat as if he was too nervous to settle back and wait. His hands kept clenching and unclenching, like he wanted to strangle someone.

"They were just with us in church," Paige said, her eyes wider than Noah had ever seen them. Suddenly he realized that she had left the house without her dark glasses—something Paige never, *ever* did.

Liane lifted her head. "Where's Larry?"

"Parking the van," Noah reminded her. "He said he'd be in soon."

She leaned back, her right hand nervously picking at the thumbnail on her left hand. "I'll be glad when Aunt Rhonda gets here. She'll know what to do about this awful mess."

"Yeah," Noah agreed. "She will."

But what could Aunt Rhonda do about *this*? She kept their lives in perfect order; so far she'd been able to handle any emergency a concert promoter could throw their way.

But not even Aunt Rhonda could have stopped that SUV from barreling through a red light. And Aunt Rhonda would be powerless to help Taz and Josiah if they were badly hurt.

Leaning forward with his elbows on his knees, Shane glanced at the big black-and-white clock overhead—ten minutes after two and still not a word from the doctors in the treatment rooms. RC had stepped out a few minutes ago to say that yes, Taz and Josiah had been brought here, but he had no other information to share.

Shane glared at the nurse at the reception desk. What was wrong with these people? If this were that hospital on *ER*, the doctors would be out here in the waiting room, spilling everything they knew for anyone to hear.

When Shane turned back to his friends, his eyes met Liane's.

"We're supposed to be on the bus now," she said, her tone flat and dull. "We should be on the road, on the way to Mobile—"

"I don't think we're going to make Mobile." He clenched his jaw, then nodded toward Larry, who sat in a chair by the water cooler. "Our driver doesn't look like he's ready to go, does he?"

Liane looked away without responding. Some questions didn't need to be answered.

Good grief, what was taking so long? Shane stood, then walked to a row of vending machines on one wall. Leaning against one of the machines, he studied the rows of chips and candy bars behind the smudged glass.

A stranger's voice cut into his thoughts: "You gonna buy something, or are you holding that machine up?"

Shane straightened and backed away. A tall black-haired man in a short white coat stood behind him. "Sorry."

The man came forward, dropped several quarters into the machine, then bent to pull out a bag of pork rinds. He backed away, then turned again and grinned at Shane. "Don't I know you?"

Shane shook his head. "I don't think so."

The guy snapped his fingers. "Wait a minute, it's coming to me . . ." A light filled his eyes when he saw Liane, Paige, and Noah sitting in the chairs. "Man, oh, man, it's you guys! YB2!"

Shane blew out his cheeks in irritation, but Liane managed a weak smile. "Yes, it's us."

"Can I have your autograph?" The man patted his pockets. "I know I have paper somewhere—"

Shock and anger burned in his stomach as Shane held

up his hand. "Wait a minute. Are you a doctor? Shouldn't you be tending to patients or something?"

The guy's smile flickered. "I'm an orderly. And this is my lunch break."

"Well—okay, then. We'd be happy to send you an autographed picture, but two of our friends were just in an accident, so this isn't a good time for us."

The man's gleeful expression faded. "Man, that's too bad. Anybody I know?"

"Our soundman," Noah said, sounding mournful. "And Josiah."

"The cute short guy," Liane added. "The one who's only been with us a few months."

"Aw, that's too bad." The man's face fell for an instant, then he looked at Shane again. "If I give you my address, could you send me about five of those autographed pictures? I have some nieces and nephews who'd love them."

Shane clenched his fist, about to punch someone or something, but Liane jumped to the rescue.

"Give me your address," she said, standing. "Write it on something I can take with me."

The man dug in his pockets again, then pulled out a slip of paper. "Just let me go to the desk and grab a pen . . ."

As soon as he was out of hearing range, Paige lifted her head. "What do you want to bet he sells those pictures on eBay?" Her voice sounded bitter. "Of all the times I haven't liked being a celebrity, this is the worst."

Shane couldn't help but agree. And a few minutes later, when the guy came back and gave Liane a card with his name and address, she slipped it into her pocket without a word.

Shane was afraid the guy might stick around and try to make conversation, but at that moment the wide glass doors opened and Aunt Rhonda ran into the hospital, her keys in one hand and a manila folder in the other. She took two steps into the open space, looked around frantically, then slumped when she saw Shane and the others.

"Hi, guys," she called, hurrying toward them. "Any word?"

Shane felt some of his frustration ebb away. Now that Aunt Rhonda had arrived, some of the responsibility would shift from his shoulders to hers.

"No word yet," he said, "but Dad went back in to check on things. He went through those doors over there—" he pointed to the swinging doors that led into the treatment area—"and he said he'd let us know if he learned something."

Aunt Rhonda looked toward the desk with worried eyes. "Did he take the consent forms I gave him?"

"Yeah," Shane answered. "They said everything was fine. But I know they'll want to talk to you about insurance and stuff."

"That can wait a minute." Aunt Rhonda fell into the empty chair next to Larry, then gave him a tired smile. "Taz's mother is on the way over," she said, "and Josiah's parents are standing by for further word. If it's serious, they're coming right down."

Shane didn't see how the wrecked car they had all seen meant anything *but* serious injuries, but Aunt Rhonda had to be hoping for the best.

The white doors leading into the treatment area opened and RC appeared again, his face drawn and pale.

"Dad?" Shane took a step toward his father. "How are they?"

"They're alive," he said, relief in his voice.

"Just *alive*?" Paige turned toward him. "What's going on?"

RC walked forward a couple of steps, then put out his hand and leaned against the wall. For a long moment he said nothing, then he whispered, "We need to pray, gang."

9

The situation was bad. Paige could hear it in her father's voice.

"Josiah is pretty banged up, but he's going to be okay," RC said, speaking slowly. "They want to keep him overnight just to be sure, but the only fracture they could see is in his wrist. The doctor says it's a good thing he is small—he was held tighter in the seat when the car flipped."

Paige felt her skin crawl when her father paused. The news he'd just told them about Josiah wasn't too bad, which could only mean the heaviness in his voice had to do with the news about Taz.

RC paused to clear his throat, then went on. "On the other hand," his voice cracked, "Taz was on the side of the car that got hit. And the doctor says he's not sure if Taz can pull through. He's suffered a pretty serious head

Taz

trauma—" her father paused as his voice choked again—"but the neurologist is in there with him now. The hospital is calling someone in the military to see if they can get Taz's father back from Bosnia."

Paige lowered her head as fear squeezed her heart. RC's last comment said it all—the government wouldn't call your father from military duty in a foreign country unless they were pretty sure you might not make it.

This couldn't be happening. Not to them. They'd suffered flat tires, bad weather, bouts of the cold and the flu. But this kind of thing happened only in movies and on TV, never in real life. And Taz and Josiah had just been with them an hour ago. Taz had sat beside her in church, and she'd had to elbow him once when the steady sound of his deep breathing told her he'd fallen asleep.

He was too strong, too *alive* to be badly hurt now.

A heavy silence fell over the group, broken only by the sound of Liane's soft weeping.

"RC?" Noah asked, his voice somber, "do you think Taz is going to make it?"

Part of Paige wanted to turn on Noah and ask why in the world he thought her dad would have an answer to that stupid question, then she realized that Noah wasn't thinking clearly—maybe none of them were.

"I don't know, Noah," RC said simply. "I just don't know."

10

Josiah winced as a bright light flashed in his eyes. People were talking to him, but he could barely make out their voices over the roar of blood in his ears.

"Ouch!" he yelped when someone lifted his arm.

"That's good, Josiah," a woman answered. "You can wake up now. We're taking good care of you."

He blinked, suddenly aware that he was cold. His shirt had disappeared along with his scoliosis brace, and gloved hands were tapping at his bare chest, sticking things on him, pressing things to his skin.

Overhead, a light shone into his eyes until one of the hands reached up and adjusted the angle.

"I needed that light," a man muttered.

"You should still be able to see," a woman answered.

Josiah tried to move his head, but some kind of board

held it in place. "Steady now," another woman said. "You wouldn't want me to miss, would you?"

Miss what?

Josiah rolled his eyes toward the right, where a woman in a gauzy cap was smiling down at him.

Somehow he got his voice to work. "What are you doing?"

"Just putting a few stitches into your scalp. Don't worry, no one will be able to see the scar once your hair grows back. You'll be charming all the girls again just as soon as you're ready."

Josiah snorted. "I don't charm girls. Shane does."

"Who's Shane?"

Josiah blinked in disbelief. Didn't these people know who he was? Did they know *anything*? And what had she meant by that comment about his hair? They hadn't . . . no, surely they wouldn't shave his head. They *couldn't* shave his head.

He stared at the ceiling and tried to figure out what had happened. He'd been on his way to buy lipstick— no, that couldn't be right. He had been on his way to buy a video game. He'd been talking to Taz, and now he seemed to be in a hospital, lying on a table. But how did he get here? He had to hurry—he had to get ready to catch the bus.

He looked at the woman again. "Where's the bus?"

She laughed as her gloved hands worked. "It's not here, I can promise you that."

"What happened?"

A man in a white coat leaned over the table from the opposite side and caught Josiah's eye. "You were in an automobile accident," he said, speaking as if Josiah were about four years old. "You hurt your hand and your head. Do you remember anything about it?"

Josiah tried to frown, but the muscles in his face seemed stiff and uncooperative. His entire body hurt, from his legs to his arms, and most especially his head.

"I was going to Target," he told the man. "I was riding with Taz."

The man nodded. "Sure, kid."

A sudden thought made Josiah's blood run cold. "Where *is* Taz?"

The woman snipped at the thread with a pair of scissors. "Your friend is in the next cubicle with the doctor."

"Is he okay?"

The man answered this time. "They're taking very good care of him."

Josiah lifted his head—ouch, his neck hurt—and tried to look around the room. He thought he saw his shirt on the floor along with his scoliosis brace, but he couldn't see any sign of Taz.

Another man came into the room, an older man who wore a white coat and had a stethoscope draped around his neck. He carried a clipboard in his hand. "Josiah," he said, smiling briefly before looking back down to the clipboard, "you have sustained several lacerations, a few bruises, and the X-rays show a broken wrist. We also suspect a concussion. But your back's in fine shape and you are one lucky young man—I think it's a miracle you both survived a convertible rollover. We want to keep you overnight for observation, but before we take you up to a room, a few people waiting outside would like to say hello."

Josiah shook his head, then grimaced at the pain. "I can't stay overnight. I have to go to Mobile."

"What's he talking about?" the doctor asked the nurse.

"Just lie still," one of the nurses cautioned. "We'll have you ready to move in a minute."

Josiah tried to relax against the table, but when he lifted his arms to cross his bare stomach, a sharp pain shot through his left arm.

He glanced at it. Someone had strapped it to a board, so that must be the broken wrist.

He closed his eyes and tried to put the pieces together. Okay—so he and Taz were in the hospital. They must have ridden in an ambulance to get here, but Josiah didn't remember anything about that.

And unless there was a new video game lying somewhere around this place, they'd never made it to Target.

"Hiya, Joe. How are you feeling?"

Josiah's eyes flew open as RC's face floated into his field of vision.

"RC." Again he struggled to lift his head. "Listen, I'm okay, so you've got to tell them to let me out of here. I'm almost all packed and ready to go—"

"Relax, Joe." RC's big hand came to rest on Josiah's

shoulder. "Nobody's going to Mobile. We canceled the concert."

Josiah let his head fall back to the table. As far as he knew, YB2 had *never* canceled a concert. Even if one of the singers got sick, RC would expect him to pull himself together long enough to perform.

He licked his dry lips. "Do you know what happened?"

"You and Taz got hit by a guy who ran a red light while he was talking on his cell phone." RC smiled, but the smile didn't reach his eyes. "The investigating officer assured me the accident wasn't your fault. You were just in the wrong place at the wrong time."

"And Taz?"

RC looked toward the door. "They're working on him. Hey, listen, Joe—I called your parents, and they'll come down if you say the word. Do you want them to be here?"

"Why would I want them to do that?" Josiah frowned up at RC. "I saw them just a few days ago. And I'm not hurt. My hand feels kinda numb, and so does my head—"

"They gave you pain medication for your broken wrist, and I'm pretty sure they gave you a local anesthetic for your head." RC whistled as he peered at Josiah's head. "I see six—no, seven stitches. You're gonna have real bragging rights when you see the other kids."

"Am I bald?"

RC coughed a laugh. "No, son, you're not bald. But they did have to shave a little section so the doctor could put in the stitches. It'll grow out in no time."

Josiah nodded. And suddenly he wanted to see the

others, wanted to know they didn't hold him responsible for this entire mess.

"Hey, RC—do you think you can talk the doctor into letting me go home tonight? I'm feeling okay, and I'd rather be with everyone else than stuck in a room by myself."

"They're all outside. You can see them, but I really want you to stay here tonight. When all that pain medication wears off, I'd rather you have a nurse handy to make sure you're okay." He smiled. "Don't worry—you won't be alone. One of us will be with you all the way."

A nurse came into the room, nodded to RC, then draped a light blanket over his bare chest. "Hi, Josiah," she said, walking to the head of the gurney. "Ready to take a ride? Some folks out here are waiting to see you."

Josiah shrugged as the ceiling tiles begin to slide away. "Actually," he said with a smile, "I'm feeling pretty good. Everything is kinda soft, you know, and a little blurry . . ."

She laughed. "Feelin' no pain, huh?"

They hadn't gone far when he heard familiar voices, then Liane, Noah, Paige, Shane, Larry, and Aunt Rhonda crowded around his ride.

"Hey, Joe!"

"How are you, sport?"

"It's so good to see you!"

"How're ya feeling, dude?"

"Josiah—I'm so glad you're all right."

He grinned around the circle, suddenly grateful for

the blanket the nurse had used to cover him. He felt like a bug under a microscope with so many people peering down at him.

"I'm good." He grinned at Liane, then felt his heart pound a little harder when she touched his shoulder. "I mean it—I'm really good, guys."

Liane looked into his eyes and smiled. "We heard you broke your wrist, so I guess you'll be singing in a cast for a while."

He lifted one shoulder in what he hoped was a no-big-deal shrug. "Hey—if I can move in a scoliosis brace, I can sure move in an arm cast."

"You're such a trooper." This from Aunt Rhonda, who looked like she was about to cry with relief.

"I hear the food's pretty good here, man," Shane said, slipping his hands into his pockets. "But if it's not, don't sweat it. You're coming home tomorrow. We'll spring you in the morning."

"Hey, Josiah." RC shouldered through the crowd and pressed a cell phone into Josiah's uninjured hand. "Your mom and dad are on the phone."

Squirming under the scrutiny of so many pairs of eyes, Josiah held the phone to his ear and spoke in the most cheerful voice he could manage. "Mom? Dad?"

"Josiah?" His mother's voice trembled with worry. "Are you okay?"

"I'm fine." He grinned up at Shane, just to prove the point. "A broken wrist, they said. And some stitches. But nothing major."

"That's good." His father's calm, reassuring voice came across the line. "But if you start feeling any strange pains, you tell the doctor, okay?"

"I'm fine, Dad, honest. You guys don't need to worry about me."

"Are you sure you don't want us to come down there?" his mother asked. "I could be on a plane tonight if you need me."

Josiah looked up—with so many friends around, he wasn't going to be hurting for help.

"I'm fine, Mom, really. But thanks for everything. I'll call you tomorrow when we get on the road."

The smiles on the faces around him faded when he said those words. After disconnecting the call, he dropped the phone to the blanket and searched his friends' eyes. "What's wrong? What'd I say?"

Aunt Rhonda reached out and patted his leg. "Nothing, Josiah, nothing for you to worry about. But I don't think we're going to be on the road for a few days."

"But we have concerts! Mobile and New Orleans and Dallas—"

"We'll see." Aunt Rhonda pulled away. "Right now we're going to let this orderly wheel you up to your room and get you settled in. By the time you come back to the house tomorrow, I'm sure we'll have things all figured out."

Josiah said nothing, but he couldn't help noticing that a cloud of gloom had settled over the others. That's when it hit him—none of them had mentioned his *other* friend. The singers had been taught to perform even when they were sick, but they couldn't do squat without a soundman.

The orderly had begun to wheel the gurney when Josiah put his hand out and looked at RC. "Wait— where's Taz?"

The director's eyes filled with tears as he reached up to rub the back of his neck. "We're praying for him, Joe."

The words strummed a shiver from Josiah. He was about to ask another question when a pair of glass doors flew open and a group of men burst through the door. "That's them," one of the men called, and before Josiah knew what was happening, the strobe lights of camera flashes were lighting the room.

"Get him out of here!" RC roared, and the orderly gave Josiah's gurney a mighty shove. Shane and Noah ran alongside, helping move the rolling table, until they had passed through another set of doors and entered an elevator.

Josiah saw Shane give Noah a dark look as the elevator doors closed. "They know," Shane said, his voice rough with irritation. "It'll be all over the papers tomorrow."

"It'll be all over the news tonight," Noah answered. For once, neither of them smiled.

The orderly said nothing for a moment, but as the elevator chimed, he pulled a slip of paper from his pocket. "Hey, guys—I know this is probably a bad time, but could I have your autograph?"

11

When Josiah opened his eyes, for a moment he couldn't remember where he was. His hand was throbbing, the side of his face felt swollen, and someone had tightened the bedsheets so much he could barely turn over.

He blinked as his vision focused. He was lying in a bed with rails, a thin blanket covered him, and to his right a narrow window let in a stream of gray morning light. A chair sat in front of the window, and someone lay huddled there under a blanket.

"Aunt Rhonda?"

Her head jerked upright, then her face brightened. "Oh! Josiah, you startled me."

"Did you sleep there all night?"

The blanket slipped from her shoulders as she lifted her arms to stretch. "Oh yeah, but it wasn't too bad." She lowered her arms, straightened her shoulders, then looked at him. "How are you feeling this morning?"

Josiah flinched uncomfortably. "A little weird. My wrist hurts a little. Not bad, though—it's more like a dull ache than anything else."

"I'm sure the nurse will bring you something for the pain." She stood, then stepped to the edge of his bed and gestured toward his left hand. "How do you like the cast? I think the blue color is really sharp. It'll show up onstage."

"Really?" Josiah lifted his hand and stared at the cast reaching from his knuckles to about four inches past his wrist. "My skin itches under there."

"That's normal, I think. But don't worry—when the cast comes off, you'll be able to scratch all you like."

Josiah tried to remember what the doctor had told him yesterday, but nearly everything about that day had gone fuzzy in his brain.

"How long do I have to wear this?"

"About six weeks, I think. But the doctor says you can do anything but get it wet, and thank goodness it wasn't your right hand." She patted his shoulder. "You'll still be able to sign autographs."

She moved around the bed, then stepped into the small bathroom. "Just give me a minute," she called, leaning out from the doorway, "and when I'm sure my morning face won't scare everybody away, I'll go look for your nurse. The doctor said you could go home as soon as they've had a chance to check you out."

While she was in the bathroom, Josiah brought up his hand to study his cast. It looked fresh and new, not at all like the casts his friends had worn in school. Every other cast he'd seen had been scrawled with notes and signatures . . . he'd have to get the others to sign his arm as soon as he got home.

A moment later Aunt Rhonda came out, running her fingers through her short hair. "I'll just be a minute," she said, moving toward the door. "Let me get the nurse, and we'll get you out of here, Joe."

"So we can get on the road?"

She opened the door, then paused and looked back at him. "Don't worry about the concerts, Josiah. Everything is going to work out."

Josiah couldn't help but worry as the door closed. He didn't know how much money was involved, but he knew promoters spent thousands of dollars for a YB2 concert. YB2 spent bucketfuls of money, too, and Aunt Rhonda did tons of work to prepare for a gig—she sent posters, ordered albums, and hired people to sell YB2 products at the events. If they canceled many concerts, YB2 would lose a ton of money.

And who would be responsible? He would. Because he'd been bored and wanted a new video game to play on the bus.

He sank lower in the bed as a dark cloud settled over him.

12

Liane joined the others in the foyer as Aunt Rhonda pulled the van up to the front door. No one had called them together, but at the sound of the van turning into the drive, RC, Noah, Shane, and Paige had all dropped what they were doing and hurried to greet Josiah.

He moved a little stiffly as he got out of the car, but the smile he gave them seemed genuine.

Liane winced when she saw Josiah's face. He'd looked bad enough on the gurney, but somehow she'd thought his bruises would fade a little overnight. But the bruise on his cheek, which had looked red and angry yesterday, today looked purple and green.

"Hey there, Joe." She stepped forward and gave him a light hug, careful not to squeeze anything that might hurt. "It's good to have you back."

The others murmured greetings too, then Josiah

Taz

managed another weak smile. "It's good to be back. But if you don't mind, I think I'd like to go to my room for a while."

"Sure, get some rest," RC said, moving out of the way.

"Would you like some privacy?" Aunt Rhonda asked. "We could move Noah into the room with Shane, so you could have a room to yourself . . ."

Because Taz wouldn't be there.

Her unspoken words echoed in the hall as loudly as if she'd shouted them.

Liane felt her heart squeeze when Josiah grimaced. "Um . . . no, thanks. I'll just go to my own bed. I'm feeling a little dizzy."

"That'd be the pain medication," Aunt Rhonda said, nodding at RC. "Sure, go to your room and sleep it off. Sleep is the best thing for you right now."

Liane stepped aside as Josiah moved past her and walked slowly down the hall to his room.

As the others went back to whatever they'd been doing, Noah caught her eye. "Do you think he's okay?"

She shook her head. "Physically, he seems to be okay. But he's got to be feeling horrible about Taz."

"We *all* feel terrible about Taz."

"Yeah—but we weren't the ones who asked Taz to take us to the store. I'm afraid Josiah's going to feel responsible, if he doesn't feel that way already. And that's got to be hard."

She looked up as the director approached, a briefcase

in his hand. "You leaving, RC?" she asked, trying to keep her voice light.

He ran his hand over the faint stubble on his face. "I'm going to the hospital to keep Mrs. Trotter company. We're expecting Taz's father to arrive sometime today."

Liane bit her lip. She wanted to ask about Taz, but she was afraid of what she might hear. They'd had no further word last night, and her sleep had been filled with nightmares.

Noah asked the question for her. "Any word from Taz's doctor?"

RC shook his head. "He's in a coma now. The doctor says his brain is swollen so it's hard to tell if there's any damage. They won't know anything for sure until the swelling goes down. He also has a broken leg, but they've already set that."

RC looked down at the floor and took a deep breath. "The not knowing is hard, isn't it? I'm trying to have faith and trust . . . but it's a lot easier to trust God when everything's going right."

Liane felt as though the tiled floor had opened up and they all stood at the edge of a dangerous rocky cliff. Was RC doubting *God*?

The idea left her speechless.

Noah wore a look of absolute shock. "RC, are we gonna quit?"

"What?" RC stared at Noah as if he hadn't understood the question, then shook his head. "We're not gonna quit. We're gonna get YB2 back on the road as soon as possible.

I've made some calls and we've got everything under control. We're going to pray for Taz and support his family, but we're not going to let this accident defeat us."

He looked at Liane, the corners of his mouth wobbling in what was probably supposed to be a smile, then stepped through the doorway and left her and Noah in the foyer.

"Wow." Noah slid his hands into his back pockets. "I don't think I've ever seen RC like that."

"Me neither," Liane admitted. "And I don't think I like it."

13

Tuesday, January 4

After a breakfast of juice, cereal, and waffles, Josiah joined the others in the rehearsal hall. RC had left a message on the kitchen bulletin board asking them to assemble at nine, but so far there'd been no sign of the man and no clue about what he wanted them to do.

When Josiah entered the rehearsal room, Shane and Noah were down at one end of the long room, silently shooting baskets. Paige was seated at her keyboard, idly playing chord progressions, and Liane sat in a folding chair, hunched forward with her chin propped on her hands.

He didn't want to look at the soundboard where Taz should have been standing, but his eyes kept drifting to the spot as if they couldn't help it. The area was neat and tidy because Taz had cleaned it up in preparation for their tour. But the tour hadn't happened, because Josiah wanted a new game . . .

He looked away as tears stung his eyes. None of the others had come out and said the accident was his fault, but they had to be thinking it. And, wonder of wonders, no one in their group had said anything to the press. The story of the accident had been all over the news last night, and *Entertainment Tonight* had done a fifteen-minute segment with interviews from the policeman on the scene, the emergency room doctor at the hospital, and two people who'd been sitting at the light when the accident had happened. All those people seemed to be enjoying their fifteen minutes of fame, but all Josiah wanted to do was crawl under a rock and forget he'd ever *heard* of video games.

He slipped his right hand into his pocket and took a couple of steps into the room. A loose basketball rolled on the floor near Shane and Noah, but they hadn't invited him to join them and he didn't want to intrude. Paige must not have heard him come in because she hadn't said hello, and Liane looked like she was in a mood and not even aware that Josiah had entered the room.

"Hey, Joe."

He turned at the sound of RC's voice. RC stood behind him with a stranger, and both of them were waiting for Josiah to move aside so they could pass by.

Flustered, he stepped out of the way. RC strode into the hall, followed by a tall, skinny man who had to be in his thirties. The guy walked as though he had springs in his shoes, but despite the nerdy walk he looked like somebody's idea of punk. He had coal-black hair, most of which had been combed into a rooster plume that rode on top of his head and dipped onto his forehead. He wore black leather pants and a white shirt with long sleeves and cuffs that dangled below the ends of his fingers.

Josiah was used to the strange dress and mannerisms of musicians, but this guy was dressed weird and he wasn't anywhere *near* a stage.

Standing next to RC, the stranger scanned the room, then a smile curved his mouth and put hollows in his pale cheeks.

Good grief, where had RC found this freak?

"Hey, gang, can I have your attention?" RC clapped until the basketballs stopped flying, and after a minute everyone in the room had turned toward the director and the odd guy.

"Thanks," RC said, sliding onto his stool. For a moment he sat there, staring at his hands, then he lifted his head and gave them a smile that looked forced. "This accident has been hard for all of us—me included. And I know you are all coping with it the best you can. I want you to know that I'm praying for each of you as well as for Taz and his family. When one of us hurts, we all hurt."

He hesitated for a moment and looked at his hands again, and Josiah knew he'd choked up.

"But if there's one thing I know," RC finally went on,

"it's that Taz wouldn't want us to stop doing what we do. He'd want us to keep going. So we will, even though it won't be easy. We're going to get back out on the road, and we're going to behave like the professionals we are. And later, when we're together, we can talk about our questions and we can pray for Taz."

He gestured toward the stranger. "I'd like you all to meet Rip Pippen. I met Rip last month in London— he was working at the studio where we laid down the tracks for the chart we'll be performing at the White House in July. I told Rip that if he ever wanted to come to the States he should look me up, and, fortunately, a few days ago he did. So I've asked him to travel with us until Taz is back on his feet."

If anything, the heaviness in the room grew heavier. Josiah looked at Noah and Shane and Liane and Paige and wondered if they were thinking the same thing— that Rip Pippen had suddenly seemed to materialize from a giant seedpod.

Rip crossed his arms and grinned. "Hello, kids," he called, rocking back on his heels. "Awfully nice to be with you blokes."

Josiah looked at Liane, who had lifted a brow. Were they supposed to interpret for this guy, too?

"I'll expect you to make Rip feel welcome," RC said, a subtle note of warning in his voice, "and you can be sure he's good. We won't have to worry about anything with Rip behind the board."

They'd never had to worry about anything with Taz

behind the board, either. So why was RC trying to fill his slot with this old English guy?

As RC walked Rip back to the soundboard, Josiah pulled a folding chair from the stack against the wall. As he unfolded it, careful not to use his broken hand, Liane caught his eye.

"He's weird." She mouthed the words.

"I know," Josiah whispered back.

Liane brought a hand to her cheek and looked at Josiah with wide eyes. "I mean, it's like Taz is already dead or something. Why did RC bring in a replacement?"

Josiah flinched when Paige responded from the piano: "Well, we have to have a soundman, don't we? Besides, it's only temporary. Taz will be back any day now."

Paige's voice held a note of anger, and Josiah knew she had been hurt by Liane's question.

"It's not like we're criticizing RC," he tried to explain, "it's just that all this feels . . . strange. How can we go on without Taz?"

"We have to go on." Paige's lower lip jutted forward in a stubborn expression. "We have contracts to keep, with thousands of dollars riding on them."

"But if it was one of *us* in the hospital," Liane answered, "I'll bet we wouldn't be in such a hurry to get back on the road. And if either you or Shane were in a hospital bed, we probably would be off the road for a *month*."

Paige's face flushed crimson. "That's not fair."

"None of this is fair, Paige," Josiah answered, careful

to keep his voice down. "It just feels weird. It doesn't feel right to go without Taz. I keep thinking we oughta be up there in the hospital with him until he wakes up."

If he wakes up.

The words hung in the silence between them, and Josiah couldn't look at Liane or Paige. He didn't even want to *think* about the possibility of Taz dying, but some part of his brain kept insisting it could happen. After all, people died every day, and hadn't the doctor said it was a miracle they survived the crash?

"Okay, gang." Moving with a brisk step toward the front of the room, RC called for their attention. "Gather around, because we're going to go through the program from top to bottom for Rip. I've written out all the cues for him, but he'll need to see you guys in action to really get a feel for this thing."

Slowly, Josiah stood and folded his chair. So . . . RC was really going to do it. Take them on the road without Taz.

As he leaned his chair against the wall he noticed that the others seemed to be moving in slow motion. Noah and Shane put down their basketballs, Liane folded her chair, and Paige stood from the piano bench so she could play the first song in her starting position.

Like reluctant puppets, they all turned to face Rip Pippen, then went to their marks on the scuffed line Taz had taped to the floor.

Behind the line, RC ran his hands through his hair as if he was distracted. "We'll run through the program once, then I'll need you all to go to your rooms and gather your things. The bus will be here at 5:00, and we need to pull out by 5:15 at the latest. Tomorrow will be a travel day, but we should be able to make Dallas in plenty of time."

Josiah nearly dropped his jaw. So they were going ahead to Dallas? That would be a huge concert, far larger than Mobile or New Orleans. Which meant, of course, that the stakes were higher. If they didn't go, they'd lose more money . . . but if Rip Pippen made a mistake that night, the entire *world* would know about it.

Josiah found himself hoping that Rip Pippen would bomb in Dallas. Then RC would realize that Taz couldn't be replaced, and he'd bring the group home where they could wait for Taz to get better.

He *had* to get better. YB2 wouldn't be the same without him . . . and if Taz didn't wake up, Josiah would never be able to forgive himself.

14

Seated in his favorite spot on the bus, Noah
rubbed his hands over his eyes, then settled back and
tried to think if he'd forgotten anything. They usually
pulled out in the morning, so he had a morning routine
that worked pretty well, but RC's announcement of a five
o'clock departure had thrown off Noah's procedure.

Toothbrush, hair stuff, underwear, socks . . . check.
Laptop, iPod, Game Boy . . . check. *Sporting News*, *Surfing
Magazine*, Bible . . . check.

He stretched out his legs, feeling more comfortable
after running through his mental checklist. Thank goodness he didn't have to worry about his performance
clothes, props, or any of the sound equipment . . . Taz
took care of all that.

An unexpected realization startled him—Taz *had*
taken care of all that. Now Rip Pippen rode at the table

in the center of the bus, studying a notebook filled with equipment lists. He hadn't said much to anybody since climbing on the bus, but Noah didn't blame the guy for not wanting to talk to a bunch of teens half his age. He sure wouldn't want to talk if he got stuck on a bus with a group of thirty-something-year-olds who looked an awful lot like Edward Scissorhands.

Noah folded his hands and looked out the window, then caught a silver reflection in the glass. He turned his head. Across the aisle, Josiah sat alone in a double seat, his Game Boy Advance in his lap. The Game Boy's lid was closed, but Josiah made no move to open it. He just sat there with the thing in his hand, staring at it as if he expected it to talk to him or something.

Why wasn't he playing? Anybody could manage a Game Boy with a broken wrist. You might have to be a little creative, but Josiah was a whiz with video games.

Noah opened his mouth to say something, then he remembered—in the hospital Josiah had mentioned that he'd wanted to go to Target to buy a new video game. The kid had to be feeling some kind of heavy-duty guilt, and the sight of his Game Boy probably brought it all back.

Without saying a word, Noah leaned across the aisle, plucked the Game Boy from Josiah's hand, then stood and slid it into Josiah's book bag in the luggage compartment overhead. Josiah didn't say anything until Noah sat back down, then he murmured one word: "Thanks."

"It's okay." Noah leaned toward the aisle. "I think I understand."

Josiah exhaled loudly. "What if my Game Boy killed Taz?"

"Games don't kill people, Joe."

"So what if my *love* for Game Boy killed Taz? If I hadn't wanted that wrestling game, we wouldn't have gone out. And if we hadn't gone out, the wreck wouldn't have happened and *Taz* would be back there on the bus, not that weird Rick dude."

"It's Rip—and you can't think like that. You'll drive yourself crazy if you do."

Josiah shook his head. "Maybe I'm already crazy. Maybe that's why I love Game Boy so much—because I'm nuts and there's something wrong with me."

"There's nothing wrong with you, Joe. Sometimes things just happen. Good things and bad things; there doesn't always have to be a reason."

"Doesn't there?" Josiah looked at him then, his brown eyes soft with hurt and questions. "I thought God was supposed to be in charge of everything. That's what we sing about, isn't it? That God's in control?"

Noah nodded. "Sure, he is. But he's not a dictator or anything, so people are still free to make mistakes. Some guys are free to run red lights."

Josiah didn't seem to buy this answer, so Noah's mind drifted to other situations he'd never understood. "Sometimes mothers leave their families and fathers walk out on their kids. People drive drunk and kill other people— and God's still there through it all."

"I don't get it, then."

"You don't have to get it, Joe. You only have to get *through* it, dude. One day at a time."

"But why?"

"Because . . . well, my mom always says whatever doesn't kill us makes us stronger."

Noah bit his lip when he realized what he'd just said. Here he was talking about killing when Taz was hovering between life and death.

Josiah fell silent, and after a few minutes his eyes closed and his head fell back to the headrest. The shadows on the bus grew deeper as the sun slipped toward the western horizon, and Noah hoped Joe would get some sleep. The bruise on his cheek had lightened to shades of green and yellow and he still had a two-inch bald streak in his hair, but Noah knew the hair and broken wrist and bruise were the least of Joe's problems. He was wearing himself out thinking about the accident.

Noah's mind drifted back to the time when his dad had left. He'd asked a lot of the same questions Josiah was asking now, and the answers hadn't come easily. He still didn't understand a lot of things, but he had learned that God would help him get through each day. He would never stop believing that God was in control, no matter what.

Noah curled up in his seat and looked into the gathering darkness. This was his favorite time of day—the time when day died and night swam up to replace it. When he was home, he loved to sit on the beach and watch the sun drop into the ocean like a ball of fire sizzling itself out in the water.

He thought Josiah had gone to sleep, but after a few minutes a voice whispered from across the aisle. "If heaven is so great, why would God want to let Taz live?"

"Because we need him," Noah answered evenly. "And because we've been praying for Taz to live. Heaven *is* great, but earth is pretty cool, too. Why else would God put us here?"

"Excuse me." Rip Pippen's British accent cut through the stillness of the darkening bus. "Would you two pipe down up there? I'm trying terribly hard to memorize these lists, you know."

Noah looked at Josiah, who had gone wide-eyed with surprise. He couldn't believe it himself—Taz *never* would have told them to be quiet. Though he was older than all the singers, he treated them with respect and would have let them talk as loud and as long as they wanted.

This Rip guy was treating them like children.

"I don't like him," Josiah lowered his voice, "because he's not Taz."

"I don't like him, either," Noah answered, grinning, "because I think he's just plain rude."

15

Josiah sat in the bottom of a Dallas Mavericks locker and watched silently as the others went through the motions of getting ready for a concert. Liane and Paige had already come in from their dressing room; they stood in the corner now as Liane helped Paige apply face powder so she wouldn't sweat under the lights.

Noah sat on a chair, his legs crossed, strumming chords on his guitar and practicing the song he always sang at the break, while Shane paced at the back of the room, dribbling a basketball with every step. The dribbling was something new—ever since Christmas break, Shane claimed it helped him burn off nervous energy, especially lately since he'd had enough of that to power a small city.

Rip Pippen stood with RC (though Taz had never needed to come into the dressing room before a concert)

and was asking RC some last-minute questions about the program.

Lew Hargrave, vice president of Melisma Records, YB2's label, had come in for this gig—another sign that something was not right in YB2's world. Lew only came in for special occasions like Christmas, new album releases, and, apparently, nearly fatal accidents.

Josiah felt his face flush. If he hadn't wanted a new video game, Lew wouldn't be here.

The ripples of his action just kept spreading, affecting more and more people. In a week or two, everyone in the world would hate him, especially if the entire story leaked to the press. So far the news reports had only said that he and Taz were in an accident; no one had asked *why* they were in the car and rushing to Target while everyone else was packing to leave. But sooner or later someone would get curious, and when they did, his secret would leak out.

He felt like an alien from a foreign and hostile planet, a monster who had taken out half of New York with one clumsy swipe of his claw. Once he and his friend Aaron had watched a movie about a girl who would one day have a baby who would grow up to be the Antichrist, so a cult of weird people tried to wipe *her* out before she could have the baby.

He couldn't get that movie out of his mind. Someone should have gotten to *his* mother and kept him from being born. After all, he hadn't done much good with his life, and possibly killing Taz was over-the-top bad.

He could almost hear Liane fussing at him, telling him that he was exaggerating. Okay, maybe a little. But someone should have at least stopped him from suggesting that Taz take him to Target for a new video game.

Why hadn't *God* stopped him? Why hadn't God stopped that speeding SUV? Where was God that afternoon—sleeping on the job?

He clutched at his belly as his stomach churned. In a minute he was going to be sick, and getting sick before a concert was never a good thing.

RC was reading the program aloud, running through the songs as if the singers had never heard them before. Josiah looked up and saw Noah roll his eyes at Liane, then he understood. RC was pretending he did this before every concert, but he was really doing it just for Rip's benefit.

Rip took the list of songs, then gave RC a confident smile. "No worries, bloke. I've got it here in my head. And what's not in my head is on the CD, right? We can't go wrong out there."

RC bit his lip and nodded as Rip sauntered out of the room, then his shoulders sagged. "We need to pray," he told the group, watching as the door closed behind the soundman, "that everything goes smoothly with the equipment. Rip may sound confident, but I'm still a little on edge."

Paige lifted her head. "I thought you said he was the best."

"Oh, he is." Turning, RC seemed to remember that he

ought to put them at ease. "He shouldn't have any problems. But you know how it is—what can go wrong will go wrong, especially before a sellout crowd like this one."

He extended his hand toward the center of the room, his usual invitation for them to pray together. The others stood and placed their open hands on top of RC's, but Josiah couldn't seem to find enough courage to approach the prayer circle. He stayed in the locker, his arms wrapped around his stomach, and after a moment RC looked through the knot of singers and caught his eye. "You okay, Joe?"

Josiah shook his head. "I don't get it."

"You don't get what?"

"I don't get any of this. I don't understand why I'm here and Taz is in the hospital, when I'm the one who wanted to go to Target in the first place. I don't understand why God would let the accident happen. I don't understand how you can replace Taz so quickly. I don't understand how all the rest of you can stand there and pray like everything's normal when *nothing's* normal and nothing is the way it's supposed to be . . ."

He stopped as a huge knot rose in his throat. In a minute he'd be crying like a baby, and he couldn't go out there with red and watery eyes no matter what. But RC would probably *make* him go onstage, because a director who wouldn't cancel a few concerts because he didn't want to lose money wouldn't think twice about putting an upset kid up on the platform—

"You want to sit this one out?" RC spoke in a flat voice.

Josiah dropped his jaw. "You'd . . . let me?"

RC's eyes had gone steely blue. "If you don't want to sing tonight, Josiah, tell me now. It's not fair to the others who'll have to cover for you if you don't give us fair warning."

Josiah wavered, his eyes flickering over the other singers' faces. Liane wore a look of sadness, Noah looked surprised, but Shane's jaw was as set as his father's.

"I . . ." Josiah's thoughts whirled. If he didn't perform, what would he do? Sit in this locker room and feel sorry for himself all night? And the longer RC thought about it, the more disappointed in Josiah he'd become. He might even send Josiah home . . . and that would be a terrible thing.

If he *did* perform, he'd be doing his best, keeping his word, all the things a professional was supposed to do. And later he could talk to RC and maybe find some answers to his questions.

"I'll sing," he finally said, standing. He placed his broken hand in the center of the circle with the others'.

His actions, like the cast around his hand, were weighing them down in many ways.

"I'm glad you're with us, Joe." RC's voice brimmed with approval, but Josiah knew the director wouldn't forget how he had nearly bailed out on the team.

Another strike against the kid who invited disaster everywhere he went.

16

They opened with "Never Stop Believin'," and half-way into the song Josiah realized it was easy to smile and sing and pretend everything was wonderful in his world. The crowd roared its approval, the girls down front waved their signs and screamed loud enough to hurt his ears, and for the length of the opening song it was almost as though no one even realized Taz Trotter was missing from YB2.

But as soon as Shane yelled "cut" at the end of the first song and the singers moved to the back line, Josiah knew this program would be different. Shane stepped forward and a spotlight lit him, then he held up a hand and bowed his head until the crowd fell silent.

Breaking the thick hush that blanketed the room, Shane told the audience that Taz Trotter, an important member of YB2, was fighting for his life in an Orlando hospital. "Taz is in a coma," Shane said, a catch in his voice as he lifted his head and stared into the light, "and I know we would appreciate it if you would pray for him. We believe in God, we believe he answers prayers, and we love Taz. So would you please take the next couple of minutes to join us in prayer for the healing of our friend?"

Josiah had seen videos of concertgoers who lit candles on similar occasions and filled the darkness with sparkling lights. What happened next in Dallas's American Airlines Center was not as photogenic, but probably more incredible. Someone flipped a switch and brought up the houselights. Instead of glitter and spotlights, Josiah looked out on a sea of concertgoers—people in folding chairs and bleacher seats, moms and dads and kids and teenagers. He saw white faces and tan faces and black faces and every shade in between—a huge group of ordinary people.

And most of them were praying. They bowed their heads, and from out of the silence Josiah heard a low murmur that grew louder as the seconds ticked by. Some of them held hands and prayed out loud, their lips moving as their foreheads creased with concern, and others prayed alone.

As he stood there, watching in silent awe, Josiah heard the still, small voice of God speak to his own heart: *Even now, I am in control.*

Josiah didn't have time to think much about what he'd heard because as the prayers continued, Noah took his guitar from its stand and came forward, his fingers gently plucking the strings. Paige joined him on the piano, then Noah began to sing part of the quiet song he had written a few months before:

"Now now now, I'm trusting heaven alone,
Now I'm thinkin' 'bout another home,
Now I'm trading in my heart of stone,
I'm trusting heaven . . . heaven alone."

Paige joined Noah on the bridge:

"Maybe you never meant to hurt me,
Maybe the future's dark and murky,
Maybe you never would desert me,
But I still miss you . . ."

And as Noah repeated the chorus, Josiah felt his eyes well with tears. He was beginning to understand. He had been thinking that God had deserted them in the moment of the accident, but he had probably never been closer. After all, hadn't the cop said it was a miracle either of them survived? And Taz wasn't dead yet. Josiah figured he had two choices—complain against the God who had saved their lives, or trust him no matter what.

Even now, God was in control of everything.

"I'm trusting heaven," Josiah whispered under his breath. "Heaven alone."

17

Liane sighed in relief when Larry took the exit
ramp and pointed the bus toward a Denny's beside the
interstate. They'd been driving nearly all day, crossing
the Southeast on their way back from Dallas, and she
was feeling a little claustrophobic from staring at the
walls of the bus. She was also feeling depressed—come
to think of it, she hadn't had a single good day since the
accident.

Oh, she'd managed to put on a happy face onstage,
and she'd tried to be pleasant with the others. But a
dark feeling of loneliness seemed to curl around her
heart when she tried to sleep at night, and the feeling
was still there when she woke up every morning. She
thought about talking to Paige about it, but her room-
mate seemed to be ignoring Taz's situation—either that,
or she was in complete denial. Paige moved through her

day as though nothing had changed, and sometimes she even stuck up for their strange substitute soundman.

Rip Pippen had only made a bad situation worse. Thanks to him, they were making an unscheduled trip home. Things had gone well in the first half of the Dallas concert until Rip had somehow managed to lose the CD containing the tracks for the second half. After Noah's song at the break, the singers had waited in the wings for their cue to run onstage and begin the second set, but nothing happened. Finally the houselights came up again, only to reveal Rip and a couple of the roadies looking under equipment, turning notebooks upside down, and generally making a mess of things.

Liane had never seen RC so upset. While the lights were up, he had walked out onstage, promised the fans coupons for a free copy of YB2's next album, and then he'd asked Paige to come to the piano and play so the group could at least limp through the remaining half of the concert.

After one song, though, everyone knew that was a bad idea. Paige's little piano just couldn't pack the punch of a full orchestra, and Liane had been relieved when RC climbed back up onstage and apologized profusely. "Due to audio and technical difficulties," he'd said, "we're going to refund your money. Thank you so much for your support."

Later, on the bus, she'd heard him on the phone with Aunt Rhonda, telling her to cancel the concerts in Phoenix. YB2 was coming home to regroup.

Rip Pippen had boarded a plane in Dallas and flown off to Nashville, hoping to make his mark in Music City, USA. Liane and the others had felt nothing but relief as the lanky Brit grabbed his suitcase, bid them "cheerio," and sauntered away.

She looked out the window and pressed her hand to the glass, welcoming the yellow Denny's sign. After Larry parked, Shane, Noah, and Paige practically ran off the bus, followed by RC and Larry. Liane gathered up the newspaper stories and reviews she'd been clipping for her scrapbook, then slid them into one of her tote bags. She stood and followed the others, then hesitated in the aisle—Josiah was sitting in one of the seats up front, and he hadn't moved.

Not a good thing. When the stop involved food, he was usually one of the first off the bus.

She hesitated by the side of his seat. "Coming, Joe?"

He looked up from the book in his lap, then shook his head.

"Why not? Aren't you starving, or have you been eating too much junk food?"

A faint smile played at the corner of his mouth. "I'm not exactly starving."

"Stomach upset or something?"

Again, he shook his head.

"Are you boycotting Denny's?"

His smile flickered, then died out. "No."

"Afraid the waitresses will pin you to the counter and pinch your cheeks a thousand times?"

He actually laughed—for a second—before his face fell back into stillness.

She perched on the arm of the seat next to his. "Then why aren't you going to eat? It's not healthy to sit on this bus all day. We still have a long drive ahead of us."

He lifted one shoulder in a shrug. "Oh, I'll get off at the rest stops. I just don't want to get off while everybody's eating. That would be too tempting."

Liane squinted at him. "Don't tell me you're dieting. There's not an ounce of fat on you."

"I'm not dieting."

"Then what are you doing?"

He drew a deep breath, then lifted his eyes to the ceiling. "I'm fasting, okay? I made a deal with God. Last night during the concert I promised to give up food and video games for twenty-four hours if God would help Taz wake up and get better. So it's not that I don't *want* to eat—believe me, I do—but that'd be breaking my word. I can't eat, and that's that."

"Whoa." Liane slipped backward onto the seat behind her. "Whatever gave you that idea?"

"I don't know." Josiah shrugged as two spots of color appeared in his cheeks. "Maybe it was when RC talked about Gideon spreading out those fleeces and asking God to make them wet and the ground dry. I'd never realized you could make deals with God, so I figured this would be a good thing to try."

Liane rubbed her nose. "I don't know, Joe. I'm not sure God still works that way."

"Oh yeah? My friend Aaron goes to a church where they have to give up all kinds of things for Lent—he gives up broccoli, because he doesn't like it anyway. We both know that's stupid, but his family believes in giving up stuff for God. So if Aaron can give up broccoli, which he hates, just to show God that he's grateful for Jesus dyin' on the cross, I figured I could give up food and video games, which I really *like*. Then God will *know* I'm serious, and he'll get busy and answer our prayers."

Liane stared at Josiah. Was he right? Along with feeling sad, she'd been feeling guilty about getting on with life while Taz was still in the hospital. Maybe Josiah had the right idea and they should all be making some sacrifices to remind God—and themselves—that they needed to pray for Taz. Because they sure weren't complete without him.

"Okay." She crossed her arms. "I suppose what you say makes some sense. So I'll do it with you."

Josiah's eyes gleamed. "What are you giving up?"

She tilted her head, thinking. She couldn't give up too much food—she'd tried crash diets before and only ended up making herself feel weak and light-headed. RC would be upset if she made herself sick.

"I'll give up desserts," she said, "and listening to my iPod for the next twenty-four hours. I'll really miss that, even though all I've been listening to lately is sad music. And I won't do anything fun."

"That's good." A thoughtful expression entered

Josiah's eyes as he looked out the window. "Why should we be having fun while Taz is sick?"

"We won't. And we won't say anything to the others unless they ask. I don't think they should do this because they're just trying to be like us. They'll have to *want* to do it."

Josiah nodded soberly. "Agreed."

18

Alone in the men's room at Denny's, Shane lowered his fists to the counter and glared at his reflection in the mirror.

It wasn't fair. Nothing was fair—not the accident, not the fiasco at the Dallas concert, not the way his father had snapped at him when he'd asked why they were going home instead of completing this tour. Even though RC had apologized later, Shane still felt the sting of his dad's words.

It wasn't his fault they were in this mess. It wasn't anybody's fault, really, unless you wanted to blame the idiot who'd been talking on his cell phone when he should have been looking at the traffic lights.

That guy ought to be strung up by his thumbs or something. He ought to be the one sitting by Taz's bed, or maybe they should have forced *him* to come on tour and help Rip Pippen try to keep things in order back at the soundboard. Maybe they should sue him for the huge financial losses they were going to suffer because they'd had to cancel concerts and refund nearly sixteen thousand tickets.

Shane drew a long, quivering breath, barely mastering the anger that shook him. The other kids didn't feel what he felt, because they didn't think much about the business side of things. But Shane had to because it involved his family, his father, and his future. Liane and Noah and Josiah could fly away on breaks and never even think about YB2 when they were home, but Shane lived with the office in his house, and his father and aunt were the very heart and soul of the business. Whatever RC and Aunt Rhonda felt, Shane felt, too.

When he thought about how long it would take them to make up their financial losses, he could almost taste his anger. They wouldn't go bankrupt, but they wouldn't be raking in the dough, either. And while Liane and Noah and Josiah were thrilled with the money being dropped into their trust funds, they didn't realize that YB2 Incorporated would take a heavy hit this year.

He could feel rage boiling just beneath his skin. He wished the driver of the SUV that had hit the Z4 would come through the doorway right now, just so Shane could punch somebody and get some satisfaction.

He balled his hand into a fist and punched at the first object in sight—the plastic paper towel dispenser on the wall. The sounds of the slam and a sharp crack echoed in the tiled room, followed by Shane's low moan as he brought his smashed hand close to his ribs.

Man, he shoulda thought before doing that. He felt as though he'd jammed his wrist bones up into his elbow. He groaned. What would the others think if he ended up wearing a cast on *his* hand?

He turned on the cold water with his left hand, then held his throbbing right hand under the stream. He flinched when the squeak of a metal door broke the stillness and a man stepped out from one of the bathroom stalls.

Shane's mouth went dry. He could have sworn he was alone—he'd checked all the stalls when he came in and didn't see any feet beneath the doors. But apparently he hadn't checked very carefully, because this guy was here and, judging by his expression, he'd heard the smash and realized what had happened.

The stranger moved to the sink next to Shane's and turned on the water. He grinned as their eyes met in the mirror. "Didn't help, did it?"

Shane frowned, then shook his head. "No," he said, flexing his red fingers beneath the running water. "It didn't."

The man squirted soap on his hands, then rubbed them together. "That's always the way it is with anger. You think you're going to get it out, but you can't handle it that way. Getting it out only hurts you."

Shane said nothing as the guy lathered up. A real

germ-a-phobe, this guy. But he was right about punching things. Shane's hand was still aching.

"So what do you do?" Shane asked.

The guy shrugged as he rinsed. "I look at what's making me angry. If it's something I can fix or address, I do what I can to take care of it. If it's something out of my control, I turn it over to the Boss."

Shane blew out a breath. "That's just it. I can't turn this over to the Boss. He's got enough trouble to deal with."

"I wasn't talking about an earthly boss." The man grinned as he stepped up to tear a paper towel from the cracked dispenser. "I was talking about God. He can deal with anything."

The man wiped his hands, wadded the paper towel into a ball, then tossed it into the trash can. A perfect shot.

"Two points," Shane said, shifting his gaze to the stranger's face.

"Try it," the man said, and for an instant Shane thought he meant he should take a shot at the trash can.

But when the door closed and Shane found himself alone again, he realized the guy wasn't talking about paper towels.

19

At ten o'clock on Friday night, when his twenty-four
hours of sacrifice had ended, Josiah couldn't wait to IM
Aunt Rhonda. He knew she'd be at her computer until
nearly midnight, and as his laptop booted up from the
Internet connection in the hotel room, he tried to act as
casual as possible in front of the other guys. He didn't
want Shane or Noah to know what he was doing—didn't
the Bible say you were supposed to be quiet about the
sacrifices you made for God?

After signing in, he sent Aunt Rhonda a quick message:

JJ91:   u there?

After a minute, she zipped back a reply:

AUNTRO: Josiah? R U OK?
JJ91:   yes. i was just wondering about Taz.

The cursor blinked for a long moment, then her answer filled the box at the bottom of his screen:

AUNTRO: He is the same. I wish I could tell u
something different, but I can't. No change.

Josiah felt his heart sink. No change? After all he and Liane had given up? Maybe they hadn't given it enough time. Maybe God wasn't noticing everything they'd sacrificed. Maybe he'd notice tonight, so Taz would start getting better tomorrow.

He typed another quick note:

JJ91:   maybe 2morrow he will improve. i hope so.
call us if he does, OK? ttfn.

He clicked off the computer as Shane entered the room. Shane and Taz usually roomed together in hotels, but since Taz wasn't here, Shane had reserved a roll-away bed in the room with Josiah and Noah.

Shane glanced at Josiah, then nodded at the telephone on the desk. "You hungry, Joe? Noah and I were talking about ordering some burgers from room service."

Josiah considered. His stomach felt like it had shriveled to the size of a peanut. He was starving, he felt weak in his bones, and nothing sounded better than a big, juicy burger and fries . . . but could he eat it with a clear conscience? Had he done enough for Taz?

He glanced at the clock again. Five minutes past ten, which meant he'd been fasting for twenty-six hours and five minutes. Surely that was plenty of time for God to get the message.

"Yeah, I want a burger." Josiah rummaged through the magazines on the desk for the room service menu. "And fries, and maybe a bowl of ice cream. Maybe I'll have *two* burgers."

Shane laughed. "Just a minute. Noah's outside in the hall, so let me ask him what he wants."

As Shane left the room to find Noah, Josiah sat on the edge of the bed and looked into the mirror across the room.

The bruise on his cheek had lightened to a pale yellow with touches of green. A light brown fuzz had begun to grow on his scalp, and he'd get his stitches taken out in a couple of days. The cast was still on his wrist, but that was nothing—lots of kids had to wear a cast when they broke a bone playing sports or something.

Anyone who looked at him would think he was a normal thirteen-year-old, not a miracle survivor. He couldn't believe it himself sometimes—and he still couldn't understand why Taz was lying in a hospital bed while he was running around doing all the things he'd been doing before the crash.

He had done everything he knew to do so God would make Taz better. He'd worked hard with the group, he'd been reading his Bible, he'd prayed for Taz so many times he felt like a skipping CD. And in the last twenty-four hours he'd given up food and fun with the others.

What else did God expect him to do?

20

Liane picked up the remote and aimlessly pressed the channel button, not caring what she watched. They had traveled all day on a boring interstate highway, and, due to her fast, she hadn't felt right about turning on her iPod, her laptop, or her pocket PC.

She'd been bored silly, and that only made her feel worse.

Paige, who sat on the bed on the other side of the nightstand, was quietly reading her Braille Bible, her fingers skimming over the pages. Liane thought about interrupting her to talk, then decided that wasn't a good idea.

Liane kept flipping the channels, catching glimpses of commercials for floor wax, air freshener, and used cars. She blew past the twenty-four-hour news station—

too depressing—and hesitated when she saw a blonde actress waving her hands at some guy wearing a confused expression.

"I just have to feel this way until I don't feel this way anymore!" the actress yelled, punctuating her statement by flinging her hands into the air. "So just leave me alone!"

Liane felt the corner of her mouth rise in a half smile. So . . . sometimes you just had to let emotions run their course?

She looked at Paige, whose fingers were still flying over the Braille pages. Liane had once picked up Paige's Bible and tried to feel the page, but all the little bumps felt the same to her. Or maybe her fingertips just weren't sensitive enough to pick up the slight variations in the raised patterns.

"What?" Paige asked, stopping.

"Huh?"

"I can feel you staring at me."

"Oh, you can not."

"Well . . . I can hear you. You were fine, and then you got quiet, so I knew you had to be waiting for me, or thinking about something. Your brain is *always* thinking about something."

"Yeah." Liane hesitated, trying to gather her thoughts. "Well, I've been thinking a lot about Taz."

"Taz is fine."

"No, he's *not* fine, Paige. He's in a coma, and do you know what that means?"

Paige folded her arms over the Bible in her lap. "I'm afraid you're going to tell me."

Ignoring the comment, Liane pressed on. "A coma is the closest to death you can be and still be alive. Technically, it's a state of unconsciousness in which a person doesn't respond to any external stimulus—in other words, if you tickle a person in a coma, they don't laugh. They don't even pull away, which even a sleeping person will do."

"I know," Paige remarked, her voice dry. "I'll never forget that night you kept tickling my nose with that makeup brush."

"Forget about that." Liane scooted closer to the edge of the bed. "A coma may last only a few days, but it can last for years. But here's the thing—if you're in a coma over a month, most of the time you'll go into what they call a persistent vegetative state. The odds that you will wake up go down. And if at any point your brain's electrical activity can't be measured, you're considered dead."

She waited for some response from Paige, some sign that the girl had finally understood just how serious Taz's condition was.

But Paige only picked up her Bible and placed her fingers on the page.

"Don't you get it?" Liane said. "Don't you feel *terrible* for Taz?"

"Right now, I feel annoyed," Paige answered, turning her head away. "Because I'm trying to read and you keep interrupting."

"Arrrrrrgh!" Liane picked up the pillow from the bed, then threw herself down and covered her head with it. Paige was her best friend, but sometimes the girl could be as thick as a plank. She didn't expect Paige to want to know all about the different kinds of comas, but it would be nice if she'd pay attention to the basics, for heaven's sake.

Liane let the pillow fall from her face as a new thought occurred. Why . . . just then, Paige had been frustrated. And angry. And before that, she'd been in denial.

She hadn't seemed sad.

Intrigued by the thought, Liane propped the pillow under her head and gazed up at the ceiling.

21

Noah opened one eye as something crashed in the bathroom. Josiah was sitting at the desk checking his e-mail, so Shane had to be the noisy one.

He sat up and looked at the clock, then ran a hand through his hair. "Man, I slept like a rock."

"Call's in nine minutes," Josiah said, not turning from the laptop. "I'm going downstairs in a minute."

"I'll be right behind you." Noah stood, then pulled his jeans from the floor where he'd dropped them the night before. They would have a marathon drive today, another long stretch for hours on end.

Josiah stood, tucked his laptop under his arm, then grabbed his suitcase from where it stood by the wall. Pulling it with his good hand, he moved to the door, then struggled to open it.

Shane stepped out of the bathroom and held the door long enough for Josiah to pass by, then he let the door close and gave Noah a twisted smile.

Shane jerked his head toward the doorway as he dropped his toiletries into the suitcase on the roll-away. "You notice anything strange about Joe lately?"

Noah nodded. "Yeah—just now he seemed . . . spaced out or something. He didn't even look at me when he talked to me."

Shane snorted. "He acted weird all day yesterday. Didn't come in to eat with anyone, didn't do much of anything. I watched him for a while on the bus—he just sat there like a zombie."

Noah slipped into the shirt at the end of his bed, then ducked to look in the mirror as he finger-combed his hair. "Maybe the kid's in love."

Shane laughed. "Who's the lucky girl?"

"I dunno. But Liane was acting weird too, and something tells me she knows what his problem is." He lifted a finger as an idea struck him, then he moved to the phone.

Shane pointed to his watch. "We're supposed to be at the bus in seven minutes."

"Yeah, yeah, I know. This'll just take a sec."

Picking up the phone, he asked for Liane Nelson's room, then grinned when she answered.

"I'm glad you're still there, girl. Hey—Shane and I want to know what's up with Josiah. Since you two are chummy, we figured you would probably know."

Her voice sounded breathless in his ear. "Man, Noah, I'm running late. My hair won't cooperate and—"

"Just tell me quick—what's wrong with Joe? Is he lovesick or something?"

"Good grief. Can't this wait until we're on the bus?"

"The bus is a crowded place. Anything you say there can and probably will be heard by everybody around, including Josiah."

"Brother." He heard reluctance in her voice, but the pressure of the clock worked in his favor.

"Okay, it's like this—he's really worried about Taz, and you know he thinks the accident was his fault. So yesterday he said he was going to give up food and video games for twenty-four hours—I think he was trying to show God how sincere he is about his prayers. He talked me into a fast, too, but I only gave up desserts and listening to my iPod. My twenty-four hours will be up later today."

Noah shook his head. "Wow. Okay, thanks for filling me in."

"Don't tell him I told you, okay? He doesn't think it'll work if everybody knows."

"Sounds superstitious to me."

"Well . . . it's just a feeling he has. So don't say anything to him about it."

"Okay."

Noah hung up the phone.

"Well?" Shane lifted his brows. "What's Joe doing?"

"You won't believe it," Noah answered, glancing at

the clock. He still had five minutes, enough time to duck into the bathroom, brush his teeth, grab his duffel bag, and sprint down the stairs to the hotel lobby. "I'll tell you while we run to the bus."

22

Noah waited until everyone settled into their
places on the bus before he approached Josiah. Joe had
taken his usual seat at the window just behind the driver,
and, thankfully, nobody but Larry was around to over-
hear. RC sat at the table in the center of the bus with his
laptop, probably analyzing the damage done at the Dallas
concert, while Shane looked over his shoulder, his chin
cupped in his palm and a gloomy expression on his face.
Liane and Paige had gone back to the bunks where they
could read or talk or do whatever girls do when they're
alone.

"Hey, Joe." Noah sank into the seat next to Josiah,
which caused the younger boy to turn in surprise. A
moment later Shane walked up from the middle of the
bus and took the seat across the aisle, then leaned over
the armrest.

"Wh-what's going on?" Josiah asked, his eyes guarded as he looked from Noah to Shane. "Some kind of ambush?"

Noah shook his head. "Nothing like that. We just wanted to talk to you."

"See," Shane lowered his voice, "we heard about what you were doing—giving up food and games and all. We think it's great you care so much about Taz, but we don't want you to think we don't care about him, too."

Josiah shook his head. "I never thought that."

"Well . . . you don't see anyone else giving up stuff, do you?"

A wry smile pulled at the corner of Josiah's mouth. "Liane did it, too. But you probably know that, since she had to be the one to tell you."

"Liane's a pushover; anyone can get her to talk." Shane grinned. "But we wanted to talk to you ourselves, try to set you straight."

"You're kind of like a younger brother," Noah added, shifting to better look Josiah in the eye. "If I had a younger brother, I'd want him to be like you. And if I had a younger brother, I'd want to help him out when things get rough. Like now."

"What I want to know," Shane leaned farther into the aisle, "is why you thought you had to give up good stuff to get God to notice you. Don't you think he notices no matter what you do?"

Josiah glanced at Noah, then lowered his eyes. "I guess he does. But he doesn't seem to be doing a very good job of keeping an eye on things. So I thought maybe

I could—well, you know, *impress* him by doing some extra things."

"You thought not eating and swearing off video games would impress God?" Noah took pains to keep his voice light because he didn't want Josiah to think he was making fun. He'd never been more serious in his life.

Josiah rolled his eyes toward the window. "I don't know. I don't really know what impresses God, to tell you the truth. But I thought doing something drastic like starving myself for a day might get his attention."

Shane crossed his arms. "Honestly, I don't think we can impress God. We're like worms compared to him. He's the Boss who can handle anything."

Something flashed in Josiah's eyes. "Well, maybe this worm needed to do something to get God's attention. And I'm sorry if I can't give a million dollars or donate a kidney—although I'd do that if I thought it would make Taz better—"

"Calm down, Joe." Noah waved his hand. "We all understand what you're feeling. Maybe we weren't in the car, but we love Taz, too. And we want to keep praying and trusting that God will do what he wants to do."

Josiah lifted wet eyes. "Even if it means Taz dies?"

Noah felt a lump rise in his own throat. "That'd be hard to take, but yeah. Even if Taz dies, I've gotta believe that it's God's will. Because Taz is a believer, he's one of God's children. And God takes care of his children, even if he takes them to heaven."

As Josiah hung his head, Noah looked to Shane for

help. Nothing they had said seemed to help—Josiah seemed even more depressed than he'd been when they climbed aboard the bus.

"I think," Shane spoke slowly, "that you don't need to do anything to show God how sincere you are, Joe. He knows your heart, so he *already* knows how sincere you are. What you need to do is listen to your heart so *you'll* know how sincere you are. You say you trust God—well, do you trust him enough to be okay with whatever happens?"

Doubt shone from Josiah's eyes when he lifted his head. "I don't know."

"I don't know about myself, either," Shane answered. "When all this first happened, I was mad—really ticked at everybody and everything. But then I realized that instead of wanting to pound people, I needed to leave it in God's hands. He's gonna see this thing through. So I'm going to keep praying, and I'm going to wait and see what God wants to do."

"That's all we can do, Joe," Noah finished. "As hard as it is for us, God asks us to wait . . . and trust."

23

They stopped for dinner in Gainesville, three hours away from Orlando. Josiah ate his food without enjoying it. The tacos and rice would have tasted great any other time, but when he thought about the conversation he'd had with Shane and Noah, everything, including the spicy Mexican food, faded to blandness.

Could he really have been so wrong? At home he knew dozens of people who did things to impress God—his aunt was always giving money to the church and joking that she was buying "stars in her crown." One of his teachers had visited the Holy Land to walk the road Jesus took to Calvary and "earn brownie points in heaven."

If God didn't want his people to do things to please him, what on earth *did* he want?

He was still considering the question when they

Taz

climbed back on the bus and prepared for the last stretch of the journey home. Larry seemed in no hurry to pull out, though, and after a few minutes, Josiah realized why—RC stood outside under a street lamp, talking to someone on his cell phone. He must have wanted to have a private conversation, or he'd have made the call on the bus.

A sense of dread crawled along Josiah's nerves. Had RC heard something bad about Taz? Maybe Taz had died while they were on the road and Aunt Rhonda had left a message with the bad news.

A few moments later RC climbed onto the bus, then paused in the empty aisle. "Gang," he called, raising his voice to be heard all the way in the back, "can you all come up here for a minute?"

Josiah closed his eyes. So it had happened, then. Taz had died despite everything he and Liane had done to beg God to save his life. They'd prayed *a lot*, they had sacrificed, they had asked an entire coliseum full of people to pray that God would make Taz well.

Josiah bit his lip as the other singers shuffled forward. After a long moment, RC cleared his throat. "I just spoke to Mrs. Trotter," he said, his voice huskier than usual, "and it's been almost a week since the accident. Since there's been no change and Taz is stable, the doctors are moving him from the critical care unit to another ward. They don't know how long he'll remain there, but it'll be less expensive to care for him there than in the CCU."

Josiah exhaled and let his head drop to the back of the seat. Taz was still alive.

"The bad news," RC went on, "is that Mrs. Trotter has to go back to her job and Taz's father has to return to Bosnia. He's going to see if he can be transferred to a post near Orlando, but it's going to take the Marine Corps a few weeks to approve the paperwork."

Josiah turned toward the window, imagining what Taz would think if he woke up alone in a hospital room. RC had said that the Trotters were spending as much time as possible with their son—one of them had been in the room at all times, just in case Taz decided to wake up. But now if Taz woke, he'd be all alone.

Josiah hadn't been alone when he woke up, and he'd still been confused and scared.

"We're going to do what we can," RC continued. "Rhonda is thinking about hiring Mrs. Trotter to do some work around the office so she can keep earning a paycheck and have her afternoons free to spend at the hospital. But, ultimately, that's going to be a decision only the Trotters can make. So please keep them in your prayers for the next few days."

RC paused, hanging his head, until Paige's soft voice broke the silence. "RC? Can I say something?"

RC cleared his throat. "Go ahead."

"I was reading my Bible the other day," she said, speaking slowly, "and I found a verse I'd like to share."

Josiah turned slightly in his seat to look back at Paige. He often saw her reading her Braille Bible on the bus—she would sit at the window, sometimes with her glasses off, and as her eyes stared straight ahead her fingers would move rapidly across the page.

"Look now," Paige read, her fingers sliding across the dots on the paper. "I myself am he! There is no god other than me! I am the one who kills and gives life; I am the one who wounds and heals."

A slight smile curved her mouth. "That's Deuteronomy 32:39, in case you're interested. I was reading the Bible and thinking about Taz because I just couldn't believe this had happened. Even after that awful mess with Rip Pippen, I still kept thinking that it was all a dream or something. Nothing felt *real*, you know? And then I read this verse, and I realized that God had allowed everything."

Josiah couldn't stop himself from asking a question. "Are you saying God caused Taz's accident?"

Paige lifted a brow as she answered. "A speeding car caused it. But God knew it would happen and it was part of his plan for Taz . . . and for us. And no matter what happens, we can trust him. Because when God wounds, he also heals."

"In heaven, you mean," Josiah answered, his thoughts growing dark. "He heals everybody there."

Noah leaned forward. "I think Paige is trying to say that God knows everything about this situation—even stuff that's going to happen tomorrow and next week. So even though it bothers us a lot, we know we can get through whatever comes. No matter what happens, God is in control."

Those last few words echoed in Josiah's heart. Hadn't God whispered the same thing to him? He was in control . . . even when things seemed to make no sense.

Not wanting to argue, Josiah turned and sank back into his seat. The verse Paige had read was anything but comforting.

24

For the first time since joining YB2, Josiah did not feel happy when the bus pulled into the driveway of the Orlando house. Aunt Rhonda was waiting on the front porch as usual, ready to give everyone a welcome-home hug, but Josiah could have easily done without the ritual. Rather than hurt her feelings, though, he walked forward and endured her fierce squeeze without hugging her back.

"Joey," she whispered, holding him tightly. "Did you have a good trip?"

With his throat too tight for words, he nodded.

Aunt Rhonda pulled away and searched his face in the yellow glow of the front porch lights. "You're tired," she said, reading the look on his face. "And you've heard the news about Taz, of course."

He tensed, afraid of *more* bad news, but she reached up and lightly patted his cheek. "Don't worry, Josiah.

We're still going to visit Taz every day, and we'll keep praying that he wakes up really soon. RC is going to take care of his family, and we'll have faith that everything's going to be okay."

Easy for her to say—Aunt Rhonda could spot the silver lining in a tornado.

"By the way, Joe," Aunt Rhonda caught his sleeve, "I've arranged for you to have your stitches out next week. One of us will drive you to the hospital, and they'll pluck the stitches out in the emergency room. No big deal."

"Okay. Thanks."

He turned to find his suitcase in the line of luggage Shane and Noah were pulling from the bays, then grabbed his bag and shuffled through the front doorway. He knew he ought to stay and help the guys unload, but the sight of Noah and Shane and RC pulling off luggage and equipment only reminded him of Taz . . . and he couldn't bear the memory.

He wasn't feeling good. All he wanted to do was sleep.

25

Tuesday, January 11

Josiah peered past the elevator's double doors, then stepped into a wide hospital corridor. White tiles gleamed on the floors; a neutral beige paint covered the walls. Just beyond the elevator, a tall, curved counter beckoned like the deck of the starship *Enterprise*.

"Over here," Shane called, walking toward the counter.

Josiah hurried to keep up. He'd just visited the emergency room, where a pretty nurse he didn't remember used scissors and tweezers to pluck the stitches out of his hair. The procedure didn't hurt, though it did pull at his tender scalp a little bit, but the way she'd smiled and complimented his thick hair had kinda made it all worthwhile.

Shane had come up with the idea of going to visit Taz. Josiah wasn't wild about the idea at first—the thought of going to Taz's room and staring at him in a coma seemed like an invasion of privacy or something, like looking at a guy asleep in his Skivvies—but Shane had insisted. So here they were on this quiet floor, without any idea of what they were doing.

A pair of nurses—a woman and a man, both in tunic uniforms—stood behind the counter, and they looked up as Josiah and Shane approached. For a minute, Josiah was afraid they were going to card him to make sure he was old enough to visit this quiet place.

"Can I help you?" the woman asked.

"We're here to see Taz Trotter," Shane said, flashing the smile that made younger girls melt. "We're his friends from YB2."

The woman's round face split into a grin. "Oh, yes. I've heard a lot about you from Mr. and Mrs. Trotter. They said we should expect a stream of company when you guys got back in town."

Josiah looked away as guilt nipped at his neck. A stream of company? He hadn't wanted to come at all.

The woman stepped out from behind the desk and moved down the hall at a quick pace, the soles of her shoes squeaking with every step. "Taz is in room 203. He's alone right now, so you can stay as long as you like. Only two visitors at a time, though, so if someone else comes, one of you will have to step into the hall."

Josiah nodded, then he followed Shane into the room.

His throat tightened when he stared down at the narrow bed where Taz lay. The young man's body seemed shrunken somehow. A needle taped to his hand ran into a vein, and a bag of some clear liquid hung from a pole and dripped into a tube connected to the needle.

Josiah had to look away. He had never liked needles, and he *really* didn't like them when they were poking into his friend.

A heavy stillness lay over the room, broken only by the quiet *beep-beep* of a machine. Josiah knew from watching medical shows on TV that the machine probably recorded Taz's heartbeat or breathing, but he didn't want to look too closely. Everything about this room made him uncomfortable and reminded him of his own short stay in the hospital. Taz didn't belong here; *nobody* belonged here. Taz needed to be back at the Orlando house with the rest of the group.

"Hello, boys."

Josiah turned in relief when Mrs. Trotter's soft voice broke the stillness. She took a minute to squeeze each of them in a hug, holding Josiah for an extra-long moment.

"You okay, child?" she asked, her dark brown eyes searching his face. "You look good. Your broken wrist giving you any trouble?"

Josiah shook his head. "No, ma'am."

"That's good, then. I'm glad to hear it."

Josiah blinked away tears as Taz's mother turned to hug Shane. Some part of Mrs. Trotter was probably wishing Josiah lay in the hospital bed instead of her son, but she was too nice to say anything like that.

"Um, there are only supposed to be two people in

here," Josiah said, inching toward the door. "You take as long as you want. I'll wait out in the hall."

He made a quick exit before Shane could protest, then slumped against the wall in relief. No one stirred in the hall, which was a good thing, or they'd see the tears that had leaked from the corners of his eyes.

He dashed the wetness away with his shirtsleeve, then linked his hands behind his back and leaned against the wall. At the far end of the corridor, a man in a white jacket was pushing a cart and stopping by each room— probably to check on supplies or something, Josiah guessed. He knew very little about hospitals and didn't want to know any more.

He turned toward the other end of the corridor and studied the painted wall several feet beyond the nurse's station. He blinked when he saw an older man approaching, a balding fellow with stooped shoulders and white hair that flowed from just over his ears to the edge of his collar. With his hands in the pockets of his brown coat, the fellow walked as if he was out for a simple stroll, but he was smiling at Josiah as if he knew him.

Maybe he did. Millions of teens knew YB2; maybe this guy had grandkids who were fans.

Josiah shifted his gaze out of politeness, hoping the man would walk on by without comment. As he turned his eyes, he looked through the doorway of the room opposite Taz's—room 204. He could see the end of a bed and a lump beneath the covers. Some sick person's foot.

He felt a prickle of alarm when the old man kept coming, then stopped at the open doorway of room 204. Looking at the floor, Josiah had the uneasy feeling that if he were to lift his head, he'd find the man staring at *him* . . .

He was being paranoid. The guy was harmless, nothing to be afraid of.

So he did look up and found the old man staring at him and grinning like he'd stumbled across his best friend. He nodded at Josiah. "You here to see Taz?"

So that explained it. The man knew Taz or his parents, so he had to know Taz's friends would come by when they could.

"I am," Josiah answered. "But his mom's in there with Shane, and you know . . ." Not knowing what else to say, he shrugged.

The man nodded toward room 204. "I'm here for Scott."

"Oh?" Josiah tried to put on a pleasant expression. "Is he related to you?"

The man laughed. "Not in the way you think. But since I enjoy serving all of God's children, perhaps our love for the Lord binds us together."

The fellow was making no sense at all, but Josiah figured elderly people were allowed to ramble now and then. He waited for the guy to go on into room 204, but he lingered in the hall as if he expected Josiah to say something else.

"Um . . ." Josiah began. "I, uh, don't think anyone else is in that room. So you can go ahead in if you want."

"I will." The old man smiled. "But I have a message for you."

Josiah nearly laughed out loud. He couldn't imagine what kind of message this guy might have brought— maybe he'd been carrying a fan letter from his granddaughter for weeks, hoping to run into someone from YB2. The word about Taz's connection to the group had to have leaked.

Josiah tilted his head. "You have a message for me?"

The man nodded, his white hair spilling over his collar in a thin stream. "The Father has sent me to tell you, Josiah, that you should not let the devil burden you with guilt for the situation that has caused you so much pain. Taz will live many more years, because he has not yet accomplished all the Lord has for him to do. So be strong and of good courage, for the Lord has heard your prayers."

Josiah glanced around, half-expecting to see a couple of men in white jackets coming from the psych ward.

"And now—" the visitor gestured toward room 204— "I must see Scott."

"Go ahead." Josiah watched as the old man walked into the room, then turned the corner and disappeared behind the wall.

What had he meant by that crazy speech? Josiah stood in the polished hallway, thinking about all of it when a flash of brightness caught his attention. The sight was brief—like the sudden blaze of a bulb that arcs before it burns out—but the light had undeniably come from room 204.

"What in the—" Josiah pulled himself off the wall and looked around. A moment later the nurses came running on their soft-soled shoes, ignoring Josiah as they ran into room 204.

Josiah peered through the open door of Taz's room, trying to get Shane's attention, but Shane was talking to Mrs. Trotter and both of them were facing Taz, not the door. Sighing, Josiah turned, then jumped when he found the old guy standing right in front of him.

He yelped. "Good grief! You scared me!"

"Don't forget," the man said, smiling his calm little smile. "Be of good courage."

Josiah took a side step and looked into the room. "Shane?"

Shane looked over his shoulder. "Yeah?"

"Um . . . can you come here a minute? I have someone I want you to meet."

When he turned again, the strange visitor was gone. Just like that. No sign of him waiting at the elevator, at the nurse's desk, or shuffling down the hall. Either he had developed the ability to run like the wind without making a sound or he had . . . vanished.

Like an angel.

26

Shane held up his hand as Josiah babbled about an old guy, a flash of light, and a message from God. "Wait a minute, slow down," he said, pulling Josiah away from Taz's open door. "And lower your voice, will you? Mrs. Trotter's gonna hear you . . . and she's gonna think you're nuts."

"But I'm not crazy, don't you see? I thought the dude had escaped from the psych ward or something, but he didn't look at all crazy. He was short, with white hair that sort of stuck out around his head, and he knew my name!"

Shane blew out his cheeks. "Millions of people know your name, Joe. Millions more know your face."

Josiah shook his head. "It wasn't like that. He didn't ask for an autograph; he didn't ask anything about the group. But he said he had a message from God—'from the Father' is how he put it."

Taz

Shane tipped his head back. "What was the message?"

"That's the good part—he said Taz was going to live many more years because he still had lots to do. And he said we should be strong and of good courage."

Shane exhaled slowly as the words rang a bell in his memory. "That sounds like what the angels said to the shepherds. Are you *sure* this guy wasn't a mental patient?"

Josiah narrowed his eyes in a glare. "I told you, he couldn't have been. He was standing right in front of me after the flash from the other room, and I looked away only for a second. I looked away again, trying to get your attention, and when I looked back, he was gone. He wasn't in the hall, at the nurse's desk, at the elevator—"

"Joe, think." Shane reached out and took Josiah's shoulders, then turned him to face the long hall. "See all those rooms? See those open doors? He could have stepped into any of them and you wouldn't have seen him."

Josiah hesitated, the light of hope dimming in his eyes, but within a moment it flared again. He shook his head. "I know you don't believe me, Shane, but it's true. I believe him. He said God has heard our prayers and he is going to answer them. Taz is going to be okay."

Shane looked up as a nurse stepped from the room across the hall. "Excuse me." He waved for her attention. "Is the patient in that room named Scott?"

She frowned. "No. This is—was—Mr. Gregory's room."

Josiah's shoulders drooped. "He died?"

The nurse pressed her hand to the back of her neck

and shook her head. "It happened a few moments ago. Sometimes people just slip away."

Josiah took a step forward. "Are the lights in the room okay? I thought I saw a bulb blow out when the old man went in there."

The nurse shot him a puzzled look. "The lights are fine. And there was no one in the room."

Josiah's jaw dropped.

Eager to step in before Josiah erupted in a stream of questions, Shane turned to the nurse. "So you're *sure* his name wasn't Scott?"

"I'm sure—his name was Gregory. He was a sixty-five-year-old man who entered a coma after suffering a stroke. I doubt you'd know him."

"You've got most of it right," said the male nurse coming through the door. "All but the name. His full name was Scott Gregory."

Shane felt a shiver run through him as his eyes met Josiah's.

"The man said he'd come for *Scott*," Josiah whispered, rubbing his arms as if he'd felt a chill. "And then I saw the light—that must have been when he took Scott's soul to heaven."

"But you said you talked to the old guy right after that," Shane pointed out. "So how could he have taken the guy's soul—"

"I don't know, maybe he travels faster than the speed of sound or something. All I know is he was here, then he wasn't. And he said he had a message from God."

Taz

Shane pressed his finger to his lips when he heard Mrs. Trotter moving toward the door. A moment later she had joined Shane and Josiah in the hall.

She paused to dab at her eyes with a crumpled tissue. "Thank you—" Mrs. Trotter's hand fell upon Shane's arm—"for coming down here. I don't want you to feel that you have to stay all the time, you know. Rhonda's been very kind about offering me a job so I can spend my afternoons here with Taz—"

"He's going to get better, Mrs. Trotter," Josiah interrupted. "An angel just told me we should be of good courage because Taz is going to live for many more years."

If they'd been sitting at a table, Shane would have kicked Josiah.

For a second Mrs. Trotter's face froze in an expression of disbelief, then her lips trembled into a smile. "Ah, wouldn't that be somethin'," she said softly. "To see my son get out of that bed and walk into my arms."

"It's gonna happen," Josiah answered, his eyes shining. "Maybe soon. But it's going to be okay."

"That'd be nice, Joe." A tear shimmered on her cheek as she turned to look again at the young man in the hospital bed. "That'd be an answered prayer."

"It will be," Josiah promised. "For sure."

27

Josiah held his good hand to his headphones
as they sang through the latest chart Disney World's
production crew had hired them to record. They were
working in the recording studio beneath the Magic Kingdom—a state-of-the-art studio in an underground devel-
opment. It could be accessed only by an elevator hidden
behind a wooden door in Cinderella's castle. RC had given
them the morning off to walk around the park, but Josiah
discovered that walking around in a hat, glasses, and a
bushy wig for disguise was hot business, even in January.
So he and Noah had opened the secret door—one of
many, they'd discovered—and taken the elevator down
to the sprawling complex beneath the theme park.

They'd spent the rest of their free time munching on
fries and onion rings at the Disney employees' cafeteria,
then he and Noah had joined the others at the studio to

record two songs for one of the new Disney shows. Josiah liked having new work to do—though their concerts were physically and musically demanding, doing the same songs over and over grew tiresome after a while. Gigs like this kept things interesting.

He was also glad RC had found a paying gig that could help fill the calendar after having to cancel so many concerts.

"Come to the land where dreams come true," Liane and Paige sang. "Come to the fountain of Wa-kee-koo."

"Wakeekoo?" Josiah mouthed the word to Noah, who rolled his eyes and made a face.

Josiah leaned into the mike, anticipating the next line. "Ride on the waves," he sang with Noah and Shane, "learn to be brave. Test your courage and enter our caaaaaaave."

They held the note until RC cut them off, then the director turned to the sound engineer behind the glass partition. "How's that, Mitch? You need it darker?"

Josiah pulled his headphones from his ears. He couldn't explain it, exactly, but he felt great and his morning in the Magic Kingdom had nothing to do with it. He'd awakened with a sure feeling that things were going to be okay. Taz might not come out of his coma today, but he *would* wake up. In the meantime, the group could work with substitute soundmen and try to pick up some recording gigs. Maybe they could take a working break and give Shane and Paige time to write some new songs. Then they could book a studio and do some really serious recording, try some new techniques, maybe lay down a ten-part vocal track to enrich their voices on tour . . .

RC frowned at the phone on his belt. "Excuse me, gang," he said, unclipping it. "My phone is vibrating."

He held the phone to his ear and listened a moment, then his mouth spread in a broad grin. Josiah paused, watching RC's face. The man had either just won a million-dollar recording contract or—

"Taz woke up this morning." Beaming, RC lowered the phone. "His mom is with him, and they've sent for his dad. He's awake, he's talking, and he's hungry."

Paige and Liane screamed while Noah and Shane gave each other high fives. Josiah stood in silence, then closed his eyes.

You should not let the devil burden you with guilt for the situation that has caused you so much pain. Be strong and of good courage . . .

How easy it had been to worry and fret and bargain and try to manipulate God. Being depressed had been easier than having courage. But God had been good to them . . . and Taz would recover. All in God's time.

Grinning, Josiah turned to slap Shane's and Noah's hands, then he stepped across the line and caught Paige and Liane in a hug.

After this, he would never stop believing that God was in control. Never.

28

Liane hitched her thumbs through the belt loops
on her jeans and looked over the concrete driveway. The
bus was loaded, Larry was in his seat, and Aunt Rhonda
was on the front porch, ready for her farewell ritual of
waving as they pulled out. They were finally getting back
on the road, because RC had promised to give them a
soundman who could handle any emergency and not lose
their CDs at a crucial moment.

Oh, they'd managed to fill their downtime pretty well.
The folks at Disney had asked the YB2 singers to record
some backup vocals for a new ride they were planning,
and that had taken the better part of a week. Then RC
had asked the pastor of a local church to come in and
spend a couple of days in what RC called "spiritual boot
camp"—just to be sure the group members were coping
with the accident.

Taz was still mending. Liane knew Josiah and Noah had thought Taz would be fine once he opened his eyes and started talking, but it wasn't that simple. First, he still had a broken leg, so he'd be in a cast for longer than Josiah would. And he'd been weak from being bedridden for more than a week, so he'd need some time to get his strength back. Liane had overheard Aunt Rhonda mention a rehab center, so she supposed Taz might spend some time there before coming back to the group.

The rubbery thump of a basketball broke into her thoughts. Noah, Josiah, and Shane were playing monkey-in-the-middle on the driveway as they waited for RC. Paige was sitting on the little wrought-iron bench by the door, her fingers flying over her laptop keys as she wrote in her computer journal. Aunt Rhonda had a distant look in her eye, but that was to be expected. She'd had a rough time of it this month, probably rougher than anybody. She'd had to deal with canceled concerts, disgruntled promoters, anxious record executives, and two sets of worried parents.

Liane drew a deep breath as the white van pulled into the driveway. RC sat at the wheel, but the vehicle turned before she could catch a glimpse of the sound engineer. RC had said they'd bring him on just for this tour; if he worked out, they'd hire him on an indefinite basis, just until Taz was well enough to return.

"Hey, gang." RC slid out of the van and grinned at Aunt Rhonda. "Everybody ready to go?"

"Everybody but you," she called, standing on tiptoe

to see the stranger who'd opened the passenger door. "And whoever that is with you."

Liane lowered her head and walked toward the bus. She didn't really care who RC had brought—he had to be an improvement over Rip Pippen, but he couldn't be as good as Taz. Whoever he was, he wasn't going to be around very long, so it probably wasn't a good idea to get to know him *too* well.

She'd taken four steps when a familiar voice stopped her cold: "Isn't anybody going to say hello?"

She jerked her head up. Taz!

The guys tossed the basketball away and ran to welcome their friend. Liane squealed and ran toward him too, knowing that Paige and Aunt Rhonda wouldn't be far behind her.

"Taz! Man, you look great! Does the leg hurt?"

"How's your head? They superglue it back together?"

"His head wasn't broken, goof head. But Taz, dude, it's good to have you back."

"You wouldn't believe how we've missed you, Taz. If you could have seen—"

Josiah said nothing but jumped up and threw his arms around his friend in a fierce hug. Taz closed his eyes and held Joe for a minute, then released him.

"You okay, man?" he asked.

Josiah nodded, his eyes wet. "I'm good now. Really good."

"Move out of the way, group, and let him give his aunt Rhonda a hug."

Liane and the others stepped aside as Aunt Rhonda closed in, wrapping Taz in a gentle embrace. He bent to hug her in return, then caught Liane's eye and lifted his eyebrows in a what-are-you-gonna-do gesture.

Liane crossed her arms and laughed. Life was good, God was faithful, and YB2 would go on.

She couldn't wait to see what the rest of the year would bring.

29

Saturday, January 29

Back on the bus, Josiah stood in the aisle and listened to the thrumming of the wheels on the highway. Life was pretty much back to normal for YB2, and last night's concert had gone off without a hitch. They had sung with renewed energy, and the crowd had responded by singing along, screaming, and waving their arms at all the right times.

Now, looking down the aisle toward the front of the bus, Josiah could see that things had settled back into their usual patterns for YB2, too. Liane sat behind Larry, her headphones on and a book in her hands; Paige was silently playing her keyboard in the next seat. Shane and Noah were slapping their thumbs against their Game Boys, and Taz was sitting at the table, studying some kind of diagram for a new sound system.

Josiah found himself checking on Taz every few minutes. He knew he was silly to worry—Taz was fine and seemed to be doing well—but their close call had made him appreciate the soundman more than ever.

"Hey, Joe." Taz must have sensed Josiah's presence, because he spoke without turning to look behind him.

"Yeah?"

"I'm not going anywhere, bud."

Josiah felt his face flush. "I know."

"And I'm feeling pretty good—even though you guys nearly hugged the stuffing out of me yesterday."

Josiah grinned. "At least Aunt Ro was gentle."

"Yeah, she was." Taz turned, grinning over his shoulder. "So—you gonna stand there all day, or do you want to sit down and look at this schematic with me?"

Josiah wasn't even sure what a schematic was, but he'd look at anything Taz asked him to. "Sure." He slipped onto the bench seat, then looked at the diagrams covering the tabletop.

"JBL sent these to us," Taz said, his long fingers tapping the pages. "We've been using Bose speakers, but this JBL setup looks pretty good. See how these woofers are smaller than what we've been using? If the tweeters are as good, we might be able to cut down on the size of our equipment, which will lower our transportation costs—RC's gonna like that. Setup will be quicker, too, which means we'll be able to schedule concerts with less time in between . . ."

Josiah propped his head on his hand and smiled as

Taz rattled on about things Josiah didn't understand. But that was okay.

Everything was okay because God was in control.

The Complete
YB2 Songsheets

Taz

Rock

Lord, you are the solid rock
The truth on which I stand
All other ground (all other ground)
Is sinking sand.
Even in the raging storm,
I will not be moved,
A sturdy stone, you are my home,
I will lean on you.

You are my rock,
My one foundation,
You are my strength when troubles shake me
And the power that won't stop.
You are my rock,
Awesome and mighty,
And I will trust in you with everything I've got,
No matter what, you are my God, you are my rock.

I don't put my faith in things
That soon will fade away,
I know your love (I know your love)
Is here to stay.
Heaven's like a mountaintop,
You've got the perfect view,
My life and plans are in your hands,
I am safe in you.

Taz

You are my rock,
My one foundation,
You are my strength when troubles shake me
And the power that won't stop.
You are my rock,
Awesome and mighty,
And I will trust in you with everything I've got,
No matter what, you are my God, you are my rock.

You are steady,
You are strong,
You have been there all along,
You're the one I depend on—

You are my rock,
My one foundation,
You are my strength when troubles shake me
And the power that won't stop.
You are my rock,
Awesome and mighty,
And I will trust in you with everything I've got,
No matter what, you are my God, you are my rock.

WORDS AND MUSIC BY STEVE SILER, DAVID
JORDAN, AND KENT HOOPER, 2003.

Y B Alone?

You say you're brokenhearted,
You say you're all alone,
Why let yourself stay in the dark
When there's love enough within his heart
To reach you . . . and hold you.
You say your life's a waste of time,
You say you're barely getting by,
Why let yourself listen to the lies
When there's love enough within his eyes
To catch you . . . and keep you.

Chorus:
'Cause I know (Yes, I know)
The source of all love
I know (Yes, I know)
Who puts the power within,
It's not (No, it's not)
The star on the TV show,
It's God,
Who created us all. . . .

You say you're looking up now,
You say you're standing tall,
Be sure you stand on solid ground,
In the Rock alone true hope is found,
And that hope . . . is forever.

Taz

'Cause I know (Yes, I know)
The source of all love
I know (Yes, I know)
Who puts the power within,
It's not (No, it's not)
Rich man counting out his dough,
It's God,
Who created us all. . . .

The One who yearns to love you,
(Why be alone?)
Is always right beside you,
(No, you're not alone),
So never stop believing,
(He'll never let you go)
He's calling out your name
(Now and forever . . .).

Chorus:
'Cause I know (Yes, I know)
The source of all love
I know (Yes, I know)
Who puts the power within,
It's not (No, it's not)
Experts who are in the know,
It's God,
Who created us all. . . .

WORDS AND MUSIC BY RON CLAWSON,
SHANE CLAWSON, PAIGE CLAWSON, 2003.

Never Stop Believin'

Young man sittin' lost by a streetlight,
Countin' out his last few dimes,
What was he thinkin' by comin' here,
What dreams shone in his dark eyes?
Young girl cryin' lost in a bare room,
Missin' folks she's left far behind,
Where is the life she longed for?
Young Cinderella must have been blind.

Hold on, he feels your broken heart's pain,
Stand strong, faith holds the key to rescue,
Reach out to love that cleanses your heart stains,
And never stop believin' . . . that God dreams of you.

Young man finds a book in a trash can,
Opens up to a promise so old,
Reads of love bigger than his heartbreak,
Reads of One who can heal his soul—
Cinderella hears a sound in the hallway,
Old woman standing at the door,
"Hungry girl, let me warm and feed you,
I know just what you're lookin' for."

Hold on, he feels your broken heart's pain,
Stand strong, faith holds the key to rescue,
Reach out to love that cleanses your heart stains,
And never stop believin' . . . that God dreams of you.

Taz

I know you've dreamed of a true love,
(He's dreaming, too)
I know you've dreamed of a home,
(He's dreamed of you)
I know you've dreamed of forever,
(You know what to do).

Hold on, he feels your broken heart's pain,
Stand strong, faith holds the key to rescue,
Reach out to love that cleanses your heart stains,
And never stop believin' . . . that God dreams of you.

WORDS AND MUSIC BY SHANE CLAWSON
AND PAIGE CLAWSON, 2003.

I'm Trusting Heaven

I thought life would sorta flow by,
I never had much reason to cry,
Until you left me alone.
I thought I'd caught the golden ring,
Life offered me so many things,
Until my heart turned to stone.

Now now now, I'm trusting heaven alone,
Now I'm thinkin' 'bout another home,
Now I'm trading in my heart of stone,
I'm trusting heaven . . . heaven alone.

We always walked together down by the shore,
I gave you my heart, you're the one I adored,
Until you said "so long."
You were the only one I could always trust,
But when you left, oh something told me I must
Look toward something else . . .

Now now now, I'm trusting heaven alone,
Now I'm thinkin' 'bout another home,
Now I'm trading in my heart of stone,
I'm trusting heaven . . . heaven alone.

Maybe you never meant to hurt me,
Maybe the future's dark and murky,
Maybe you never would desert me,
But I still miss you. . . .

Taz

Now now now, I'm trusting heaven alone,
Now I'm thinkin' 'bout another home,
Now I'm trading in my heart of stone,
I'm trusting heaven . . . heaven alone.

WORDS AND MUSIC BY NOAH DUDASH,
ARRANGED BY PAIGE CLAWSON, 2003.

Go Vertical!

Lord, sometimes I get confused
With all I hear and see
Choices come from every side
They push and pull on me.
Help me to
Look up to you
And in everything I do—

Go Vertical—
Trusting in your plan for me.
Go Vertical—
Always looking for your will
Every single prayer I pray is a miracle
Go Vertical.

There are times when friends want me
To do something that's wrong
Lord, I need you in my heart
To help me to be strong.
Be my guide
And send your Light
So that all will know that I

Go Vertical—
Trusting in your plan for me.
Go Vertical—
Always looking for your will

Taz

Every single prayer I pray is a miracle
Go Vertical.

Come and be
Alive in me
'Cause I want to faithfully

Go Vertical—
Trusting in your plan for me.
Go Vertical—
Always looking for your will
Every single prayer I pray is a miracle
Go Vertical.

Go Vertical—
Lifting up my life to you.
Go Vertical—
Raising up my voice in praise
Every single prayer I pray is a miracle
Go Vertical.

WORDS AND MUSIC BY STEVE SILER,
KENT HOOPER, AND HENRY SILER, 2003.

Your Word

Everybody's got a word they want to sell me
Yakety-yak on my TV,
Video, radio, quadraphonic stereo,
PC, CD, DVD,
But the word that counts in my soul's survival
Is the word of truth in your holy Bible—

Your word, your word,
Your word is a lamp unto my feet,
Your word, your word,
Is a shining light that's leading me,
Your word (whose word?), your word,
Your word is a lamp unto my feet,
Your word (whose word?), your word,
Is the word I really need to read.
I need to heed your word.

Everybody's got a mouth and gums are flapping,
Blah-ba-dee-blah into my head,
Pull me left, pull me right,
Stand up, sit down, fight, fight, fight,
I'll trust in your voice instead,
'Cause the word of guidance I should follow
Is the word of life in the holy gospel.

Your word, your word,
Your word is a lamp unto my feet,

Taz

Your word, your word,
Is a shining light that's leading me,
Your word (whose word?), your word,
Your word is a lamp unto my feet,
Your word (whose word?), your word,
Is the word I really need to read.
I need to heed your word.

WORDS AND MUSIC BY STEVE SILER
AND NICK TREVISICK, 2003.

Come On (It's Time to Take Your Stand)

We are the music makers,
We are the dreamers of dreams,
We are the future's caretakers,
Come be a part of our team.

Some people ask us why we spend our time,
Singing songs with occasional retro themes,
They can't seem to feel the rhythm and rhyme,
There's an ancient pulse behind everything,
Life's greatest gifts are as old as the sky,
Love and laughter come to us from above,
Every good and great thing that meets the eye,
Spills from the bounty of the Father's love.

We (we) want to reach back into the past,
Grab what is good and celebrate life,
We (we) want to make the good things last,
Use them to reflect the True Light.
So come on and take me by the hand,
Come on, it's time to take your stand,
Come on, I'll lead you into the land
Where dreams become reality . . .

City street newsboy yells out the bad news,
CNN broadcasts grief, gloom, and despair,
People hunker down behind their closed doors,

Taz

Been so long since they have lifted a prayer,
God's still great and he is still on his throne,
Evil can never gain the upper hand,
If we call out we'll get a clear dial tone,
God's line is faster than the hottest broadband . . .

We (we) want to reach back into the past,
Grab what is good and celebrate life,
We (we) want to make the good things last,
Use them to reflect the True Light.
So come on and take me by the hand,
Come on, it's time to take your stand,
Come on, I'll lead you into the land
Where dreams become reality . . .

WORDS AND MUSIC BY SHANE CLAWSON
AND PAIGE CLAWSON, 2003.

¿Porque sé lo sé?

Tú dices que tienes el corazón en pedazos,
Tú dices que estás sola,
¿Por qué te quedas en la oscuridad?
Cuando hay amor en Su corazón
Para tocarte . . . y para abrazarte.
Tú dices que tu vida es una pérdida de tiempo,
Tú dices que apenas puedes vivir.
¿Por qué escuchas esas mentiras
Cuando hay amor en Sus ojos
Para atraerte . . . y guardarte?

Porque sé (sí, lo sé),
Quien es la fuente de amor
Y lo sé (sí, lo sé)
Quien nos brinda el poder.
No lo es (no, no es)
La estrella de TV
Es Dios . . .
Quien a todos creó.

Tú dices que todo te va bien ahora,
Tú dices que eres fuerte.
Asegúrate de que estás parada en tierra firme.
Sólo en la Roca te encuentras la esperanza,
Y esa esperanza es . . . para siempre.

Porque sé (sí, lo sé)
Quien es la fuente de amor

Taz

Y lo sé (sí, lo sé)
Quien nos brinda el poder.
No lo es (no, no es)
El rico y su dinero,
Es Dios . . .
Quien a todos creó.

Es El quien desea amarte
(¿Por qué estás sola?)
Siempre está a tu lado
(Nunca estás sola)
Nunca dejes de creer
(El nunca te abandona)
El te llama por tu nombre
(Hoy y para siempre).

Porque sé (sí, lo sé),
Quien es la fuente de amor
Y lo sé (sí, lo sé)
Quien nos brinda el poder.
No lo es (no, no es)
Los expertos del mundo,
Es Dios . . .
Quien a todos creó.

Ready for more?

Other items available in the Young Believer product line:

Young Believer Case Files

Be sure to check out
www.youngbeliever.com

How easy is it to live out your faith?

Sometimes it may seem as though no one is willing to stand up for God today. Well, *Young Believer Case Files* is here to prove that's simply not true!

Meet a group of young believers who had the guts to live out their Christian faith. Some of them had to make tough decisions, others had to hold on to God's promises during sickness or some other loss, and still others found courage to act on what God says is right, even when other people disagreed.

You can have the kind of powerful faith that makes a difference in your own life and in the lives of people around you.

The question is . . . how will YOU live out your faith?

Young Believer 365

Be sure to check out
www.youngbeliever.com

365?? You mean every day??
You'd better believe it!

Maybe you know something about the Bible . . . or maybe you don't. Maybe you know what Christians believe . . . or maybe it's new to you. It's impossible to know everything about the Bible and Christianity because God always has more to show us in his Word. *Young Believer 365* is a great way to learn more about who God is and what he's all about.

Through stories, Scripture verses, and ideas for how to live out your faith, this book will help you grow as a young believer. Experience God's power each day as you learn more about God's amazing love, his awesome plans, and his incredible promises for you.

Start today. See what God has in store for you!

Young Believer™ BIBLE

NEVER STOP BELIEVING!

Have you ever wondered why Christians believe what they do? Or how you're supposed to figure out *what* to believe? Maybe you hear words and phrases and it seems like you're supposed to know what they mean. If you've ever thought about this stuff, then the *Young Believer Bible* is for you! There isn't another Bible like it.

The *Young Believer Bible* will help you understand what the Bible is about, what Christians believe, and how to act on what you've figured out. With dozens of "Can You Believe It?" and "That's a Fact!" notes that tell of the many crazy, miraculous, and hard-to-believe events in the Bible, hundreds of "Say What??" definitions of Christian words you'll hear people talk about, plus many more cool features, you will learn why it's important to . . . **Never stop believing!**

NEW LIVING TRANSLATION®

TYNDALE KiDS

Winnie the Horse Gentler Series:

Collect all eight books!

Get to know Winnie and Lizzy, plus all of their friends, horses, and more at winniethehorsegentler.com!

Check out all these fun features:

★ Post your own stories and photos of your pet

★ Trivia games

★ Articles by the author

★ Advice on pet care

★ And much more!

mars
DIARIES
are you ready?

Set in an experimental community on Mars in the years 2039–2043, the Mars Diaries feature teen virtual-reality specialist Tyce Sanders. Life on the red planet is not always easy, but it is definitely exciting. As Tyce explores his strange surroundings, he also finds that the mysteries of the planet point to his greatest discovery—a new relationship with God.

MISSION 1: OXYGEN LEVEL ZERO
Time was running out...

MISSION 2: ALIEN PURSUIT
"Help me!" And the radio went dead....

MISSION 3: TIME BOMB
A quake rocks the red planet, uncovering a long kept secret....

MISSION 4: HAMMERHEAD
I was dead center in the laser target controls....

MISSION 5: SOLE SURVIVOR
Scientists buried alive at cave-in site!

MISSION 6: MOON RACER
Everyone has a motive...and secrets. The truth must be found before it's too late.

MISSION 7: COUNTDOWN
20 soldiers, 20 neuron rifles. There was nowhere to run.
Nowhere to hide...

MISSION 8: ROBOT WAR
Ashley and I are their only hope, and they think we're traitors.

MISSION 9: MANCHURIAN SECTOR
I was in trouble...and I couldn't trust anyone.

MISSION 10: LAST STAND
Invasion was imminent ... and we'd lost all contact with Earth.